I must remember.

I must know my name. People always know their names. So what's my name? Come on, don't get all worked up and silly, just think of your name!

She touched her throat.

No necklace.

No locket, no cross, no crystal, no delicate gold chains.

She wore no earrings. She touched her face and hair. The hair was long enough to pull forward and inspect. Deep rich brown, glinting with sun-dye. Like her hands, the hair seemed to belong to somebody else.

Okay. No clues there. Think about what's around you. Place yourself. You'll remember things once you see where you are.

Other Scholastic books
you will enjoy:

Forbidden
by Caroline B. Cooney

Saturday Night
by Caroline B. Cooney

The Party's Over
by Caroline B. Cooney

Winter Dreams, Christmas Love
by Mary Francis Shura

The Last Great Summer
by Carol Stanley

A Winter Love Story
by Jane Claypool Miner

Unforgettable

CAROLINE B. COONEY

SCHOLASTIC INC.
New York Toronto London Auckland Sydney

ISBN 0-590-47877-X

12 11 10 9 8 7 6 5 4 3 2 1 4 5 6 7 8 9/9

Printed in the U.S.A. 01

First Scholastic publishing, August 1994

Unforgettable

Chapter 1

Back home, people said she was breathtakingly beautiful. A work of art. A real show stopper.

Here in the first major city she'd ever visited, however, traffic had failed to stop for her. As far as she could tell, the trucks and buses, taxis and limousines, beat-up old sedans and fine imported cars, never even saw her. People drove like maniacs, each bumper only inches away from the next, fast as race cars, jumping lights long before they went green, and going through lights long after they'd turned red.

She didn't mind.

How wonderful to be anonymous for a change. No small town knowledge swarming around. Nobody in this entire metropolis knew her. She might never even have had a name.

I'm here! she thought, falling in love with the noise and the chaos. I'm urban. I'm city. I'm street. No more country. No more farm. No more ordering from catalogs just because there aren't any stores. From now on, my life will be crowds and taxis, skyscrapers and subways, fabulous boutiques and rich-people department stores.

And secrets, of course. She loved a good secret. Just being here was a secret. Everybody thought she was somewhere else.

Well, I'm not! she said to herself. She wanted to laugh out loud and maybe hug a stranger.

But she was trying to be intelligent. This was her first day in her first city and she didn't want to be too much of a tourist. Hugging strangers was out. Although a very cute stranger stood across the street from her. He was selling T-shirts from a wooden wagon. The boy was his own perfect ad. Clearly into bodybuilding, and not wanting to hide his great muscles, he was wearing a T-shirt that was one size too small, instead of the fashionable two sizes too large. Definitely a candidate for romance, especially since his T seemed to sport a Harvard University logo.

How she wanted a worthy boyfriend! All life would interest him, not just trucks and stereo systems. He'd be relaxed about world travel and city subways. He'd have credit cards. With a big limit.

The boys back home — oh, come on. They'd never left *town,* never mind the state. They didn't want to conquer the world. They didn't even want to pump gas.

Yes, she was willing to have a world-class romance with a Harvard boy. Not that romance meant just boys. Adventure was part of romance. Intrigue and wild crazy behavior. Furthermore, romance had to happen in a great place. Romance wasn't McDonald's. Romance wasn't the high school cafeteria. Romance was yachts and nightclubs and first-class travel on jets.

Actually, at this moment, she was lost. It didn't matter, because there were so many people waiting on the sidewalk for the WALK light that she was just a piece of crowd. Nobody would suspect she had no idea what she was doing. At least, she *hoped* nobody suspected. How humiliating if everybody took one look and said — *Beginner. Novice. Pathetic. Knows nothing about cities or anything else on earth*.

She wanted to turn sophisticated in a fingersnap. No embarrassment. No fumbling. Certainly not in public.

She knew how she looked in public right now.

She looked terrific.

Taupe linen shorts, rather long, pleated and belted. Tailored white shirt, starched and ironed. It was a nice combination of dressy and casual. Her slim athletic legs were deeply tanned. Her hair, too heavy to swing, rested on her shoulders. Bleached by hours in the sun, its dark brown was burnished like new copper or old gold.

Traffic might not stop, but the people around certainly noticed her. Little girls knew they wanted to look just like that when they grew up, and older women remembered wistfully when they *had* looked just like that.

I've got the looks, she thought, giggling. All I need now is sophistication. I have none. I grew up in the wrong place.

Hiding the giggle was probably the first step. Sophisticated young women, when walking alone, kept their features under control. They didn't giggle and they certainly didn't gape in touristy awe. Although, as she crossed this half of the street and waited on the traffic island to cross the next, she was tempted.

A magnificent hotel, its facade a glittering profile of hot red brick and slanted glass, was between her and a stretch of water so blue it looked like new jeans. THE JAYQUITH, said the sign. Guests passed in and out a thick glass door held by a doorman who seemed to be a member of some ancient army, he was so covered in scarlet and gold and striping and medals.

Oh, to stay in such a hotel! Presidents probably stayed there, and diplomats and divorcing movie stars.

She fingered the linen drawstring bag she carried, a perfect match to her shorts, but wrong, wrong, wrong, for the city. First, she didn't have enough money in it to stay at The Jayquith. Second, city women were carrying handbags of leather. Their purses closed tight as security doors over their possessions, whereas hers hung open.

Office buildings flanked the hotel. Business people strode in and out. The men wore fine suits, somehow remaining elegant and dashing in the July heat, while the tourists who stumbled around were sweaty and tired.

And the women — how wonderfully city businesswomen dressed! Mostly in black, but not plain old, drab old black, like back home. Dramatic urban black. This year's black, not last year's. The women wore high heels, and vivid jewelry, and their hair had been done. They had a way of looking at nobody. Stalking forward as if there were not hundreds of other people around. As if the sidewalks and the city were their own private property.

She wanted a city for her own private property.

The jewelry was remarkably heavy. Each emerald and ruby was larger than Kaytha's thumb. Kaytha stroked the necklace. She loved taking it out and staring at it.

Once she had tried it on, but it was no pleasure to wear. She felt like an ox with a yoke of solid gold on her neck.

Only a head of state would ever have worn such a thing. It was a Weight. A Treasure. In fact, the necklace had been Queen Isabella's. The Queen had expected Christopher Columbus to bring back armloads of such necklaces, but he of course screwed up and found nothing but the New World.

There was no jewelry like this on the face of the earth.

Kaytha smiled and touched her crystal, a slender rose pink that gleamed softly in the hollow of Kaytha's throat. A crystal on a silk cord would have been more fun for Queen Izzy.

Kaytha said, "Are we all set, Cousin Edie?" She was thinking of the gala party on the yacht, the moment for which they had been planning for so long.

"No, we are not!" said her cousin. Edie was trembling and wild-eyed.

Kaytha stared at Edie. Of course they were all set. They had been set for months. It was just a matter of waiting till Tuesday. Kaytha didn't even know why she'd asked the question, except to fill time.

Cousin Edie, lips pressed together with emotion, was staring at the surface of the coffee table. The table was a thick slab of marble, green as sea foam, and polished to a mirror shine. The necklace was doubled by its reflection. Edie's thin, pale face reflected up like an old plate.

"It's wrong!" cried Edie, and she actually wrung her hands and clutched her heart.

Edie was a mess.

Torn jeans, sagging sweatshirt. Platinum-dyed hair in need of a touch-up. Glasses far too large for a small face. What had turned Edie into such a hag? They'd better not have Edie around during the Party. What might Edie say?

Cousin Edie had been brought into the picture as Kaytha's tutor. Sometimes Kaytha went to school, depending on where they were, and how long they would be staying.

She'd gone to school in London and in Buenos Aires, but in Hong Kong she wasn't in the mood, and here in the States, she had no interest at all. If you felt like reading, you could buy a book in any airport shop, Kaytha reasoned. So why attend some institution in order to be handed the books they chose? Except for making friends, Kaytha could see no point in school. At her last two schools, Kaytha had failed to make friends anyway.

She certainly hadn't made friends with Cousin Edie.

Kaytha stared out the window and wondered what to do about Cousin Edie. It was crunch time, and Edie was collapsing. Not good.

Their suite on the seventh floor of The Jayquith looked down on tourists who were dumped by the busload: dozens and dozens of buses. Kaytha could not imagine what would bring people to Boston. It was not a city that compared, say, to Paris or San Francisco. But out they poured, from Kaytha's height nothing but hair, bald spots, and the bills of baseball caps.

Kaytha loved looking down on people. That was where people belonged. Below Kaytha.

She feasted her eyes on the T-shirt god, a

college boy with a sort of Conestoga wagon filled with stacks of Boston icons: Tea Party, Paul Revere, Harvard University. Kaytha didn't think much of his brains — selling T-shirts for a living — but on the other hand, when you looked like that, who needed brains?

Yesterday, when Kaytha purchased her eleventh T-shirt from him, he had bought her a Coke. She knew his name now. Mitch. How American. She wanted Mitch to fall in love with her. She wanted this fine, broad-faced, broad-shouldered, blond, American boy to be her property.

How fascinated Mitch must be by her . . . this unusual girl who materialized every day. If he knew how unusual Kaytha *really* was . . . !

She gloated, afloat in the mauve and silver decor of the suite. She had more secrets than any of those fools in the street. And they would never know. They would struggle along in their pitiful little facsimiles of life, and she, Kaytha, would always be above them.

Susan, although every time she needed money she promised herself that this time she would not waitress, was waitressing. The thing about waiting tables was, it was so hard.

And it was rarely fun. Susan liked stuff that was fun and easy. Acquiring money never seemed to fall into those categories.

Susan was a quarter inch under five feet. She usually counted the fluff of her hair and pretended to be five one. She was not teeny small; she did not wear size three. She was curvy, solid small. She was eighteen, looked twelve, and people invariably said to her, You're so cute. What college girl wanted to be *cute* when the competition was striking, elegant, or stunning?

She had spent her entire life staring up at people. Mitch, who was six two, required extra tilt. Susan felt she should get points for putting her neck at so much risk, but Mitch didn't notice these things.

Mitch, thought Susan longingly. He actually made her heart ache, as if she could take a medicine for him, something to absorb the crush molecules and let her sleep without fantasizing about him.

She had to go and have a crush on a guy who looked like he sold those T-shirts of his between river-rafting expeditions. He looked like a man who owned oil derricks and experimented with cold fusion when he was not riding his Harley. Almost every day, some girl or young woman asked Mitch to pose with her.

Mitch thought it was funny and always cooperated. Susan didn't think it was so funny. She knew what those girls were going to pretend when they got home — *and here's the boy I hung out with, we had the best time.*

Susan's restaurant was right on the wharf, and if she were to go out the front door, and jump up on one of the stone ledges that kept tourists from falling into the harbor, she would see Mitch. Probably see him with some beautiful girl.

Susan touched the tiny gold locket caught between her shirt and her apron. It was empty. She wanted Mitch's picture there, and she actually had quite a few snapshots of him, but unless he gave her his photograph, it didn't count. Susan had never wanted anything in her life as much as she wanted to count with this boy.

I'm no different from the lonely, desperate tourists, she thought, remembering extra sour cream for table eleven. I'm just pretending Mitch is my boyfriend. He's marking time with me, and the minute he finds perfection, which I'm not, he'll move on.

She thought she could not bear it if Mitch McKenna found somebody else. She would kill him. Or the somebody else.

* * *

Kaytha never tired of hotels. The Jayquith met Kaytha's standards. She had previously stayed in the New York Jayquith, and the Boston version, if anything, surpassed it.

Kaytha had rarely lived in a house and did not know how people could put up with the boredom of houses. A house was always in the same place. What kind of person could stand being in the same place every night?

Most of the world, evidently.

Furthermore, in houses you had to do things. There were kitchens, there were appliances, there were laundry rooms. Ugh. Kaytha did not approve of doing things. Things must be done *for* her. Hotels understood this.

Cousin Edie was drooping over the necklace. She had been quite tiresome about the necklace. Cousin Edie did not understand how much money it took to live in places like The Jayquith and was just beginning to understand where the money came from.

Kaytha wondered what to do about Edie. Should she tell how borderline Edie was getting?

The grown-ups didn't consider her one of them. They were always reminding her of Last Year, and saying she had to Prove Herself. They told her to leave the room when things got interesting. They didn't think Kaytha knew all the plans.

Kaytha always knew all the plans.

They had their secrets . . . and she had hers *and* theirs.

Kaytha laughed to herself, and did a little dance by the window, thinking of how she would have Mitch, and also the money, and . . .

. . . and when she completed her pirouette, Cousin Edie, and the necklace, were gone.

A stretch limousine, slate gray, with shadowed windows, crept out of the underground parking lot of The Jayquith. Slowly and relentlessly it moved through the traffic. It seemed to have more abilities than the other vehicles: a sort of reptile's intelligence, which enabled it to snake through jams that halted ordinary cars.

She ran long slim fingers through her bronze hair, curling it under, while she watched the limousine approach.

Wouldn't it be neat to have a limo? And gray seemed such a sophisticated choice. White was a little too Rented-Senior-Prom. Black was a little too Funeral. But gray was Substance and Wealth and Success.

She had, of course, missed the WALK light

as she stared, and was now stranded on the long thin traffic island.

People sifted themselves on the big historic plaza like ingredients for a huge sheet cake. Exhausted families and shrieking summer campers on a field trip, cuddling honeymooners and confused foreign tourists studying maps. The campers, who looked about twelve, were finishing hot dogs and arguing with their counselor, who looked about thirteen.

When she got her next summer job, it would not be as a camp counselor. She was done with the outdoors. She was going inside. A stock brokerage, perhaps. That sounded city. Maybe a law firm. Nothing sticky. No waitressing. Nothing frantic or sweaty. She would wear black, too, perhaps with a crimson scarf, like the woman now leaving The Jayquith. She herself had better legs.

The limousine also waited for the light to turn. She tried to see in the windows, but the glass had been designed to prevent that. What is it like inside a limo? she wondered.

A remarkably thin camper was hoisting her videocam, shrieking in a remarkably thin and high voice, "Everybody line up with your new T-shirts, I'm going to film you."

When I'm filmed next, she told herself, it

won't be on a home video for parents' night. I'm going to be on the news. People will be fascinated by me and always asking for interviews, and sometimes I'll grant them, but mostly I'll say no, because I'll be far too busy with my social life.

A woman had darted out of The Jayquith and raced across the street without waiting for any WALK light. What courage!

She hoped nobody would hit the woman. Boston drivers looked as if hitting people was their hobby, and this extremely busy street was prime people-hitting territory.

The woman was not attractive. Half her face was covered by ridiculously large and ugly sunglasses and the other half by a messy mop of platinum hair in need of retouching. She wore torn jeans and a big old sweatshirt.

The beautiful girl was quite disappointed. Surely people who stayed at The Jayquith ought to dress better than that.

The woman zigzagged as she ran, as if trying to escape bullets. She cast terrified, or perhaps angry, glances over her shoulder.

The girl from the country watched as if seeing a television show. Her attention was caught again by the gray limousine, whose back passenger door was suddenly flung open — the traffic-side door, not the sidewalk side where bellboys were poised to assist. Odd. What was — ?

When Torn Jeans hurled herself on top of the girl, she was completely unprepared. She wasn't standing strong, she wasn't holding onto anything, she wasn't thinking in terms of protecting herself. Torn Jeans seized her limp linen drawstring bag.

She's robbing me? But I have nothing.

Mouth contorted with emotion, Torn Jeans said something. Something desperate. Something terribly important. But there was too much traffic. Nothing could be heard.

Except for one sound: a sound the dark-haired girl knew well in the country, but in her innocence had not connected with the city.

The sound of a gunshot.

From the limousine catapulted a man who moved so quickly there was no identifying him, no focusing on him. He actually picked up Torn Jeans and threw her into the limo, leaping in on top of her, and slamming the door after himself.

The girl had lost her balance. She cried out, trying to grab the post of the WALK light. She missed.

There was a glimpse of red fender and

chrome bumper. Brakes screamed literally in her ear.

No — a dumb car accident? — I have to have a life — you can't take life away yet — I have plans — I'm only seventeen!

But gravity failed to listen to a tourist's plans for life, no matter how beautiful the tourist. She fell anyway, while the gray limousine vanished into the smoggy traffic as easily as a snake going beneath the water.

I know something you don't know.

Kaytha loved those notes. No verse in the world compared. You sang your song, you were superior. There was nothing — nothing in the world! — like a secret.

They thought they knew everything.

They thought they had covered every base and every angle.

Well, they were wrong.

For just a minute, she did nothing about it.

Savored the power. Savored knowing what Edie was going to do, and how much it would damage them all.

But in the end, she picked up her phone and quickly dialed. They were leaving on a different errand, but had their cellular phones. Plenty of time to save the day.

Besides, now they would owe her. Kaytha liked it when people owed her.

The crowds never thinned. Crowds in July never did. A drive-by shooting, and nobody said, Gee, maybe I should get out of here.

Mitch McKenna must have sold a million T-shirts. There was nothing like a major crime to make people want a souvenir.

An amazing number of people had wanted to talk to the police. This was not an occasion where nobody noticed. It was, however, an occasion where nobody agreed. Some little camper had taken a video, which might help the police, but so far, nobody knew anything. The limousine just blended into traffic and vanished.

Nobody had gotten the plate numbers. Everybody's version of what happened conflicted with everybody else's. Some people said it was a middle-aged woman and some people said it was a teenage girl with glittery hair (except for the people who said she had black hair) and some people said it was a man in a blue blazer. Nobody knew who shot whom.

Whatever it was happened in thirty seconds and was over.

Mitch had not flung himself to the pavement when he heard the gunshot only because shock froze him in place. A stack of cotton knit was not going to protect him from bullets. Mitch liked to think he was too tough for shock. Any old thing could happen, and he'd shrug, because there was nothing he hadn't seen.

But this had not been any old thing. The victim had been scooped up by the very person who'd shot at her! That was one version anyway. Another version said the shot came from the street, and the limousine rescued her.

A drug deal gone wrong if he'd ever seen one. Mitch, on the waterfront, surrounded by thousands of mingling, moving human beings, had seen quite a few. Depending which corner of the city you were in, a limousine meant a wedding or else drugs.

The plaza where he parked his T-shirt wagon was a jewel of the city. Brick and granite walkways turned into wharves which extended far out into Boston Harbor. The displays of a hundred tiny shops and restaurants glittered in the sun. The salty wind gave some relief from the midday heat.

It was not pleasant to think of the number of innocent people who could have been hit by that bullet. But evidently, not even the victim had been hit; there was no blood.

The day moved on. T-shirts moved, too.

The sun grew hotter. Heat reflected off

water, office buildings, pavement, and brick. They were imprisoned by July.

Mitch discussed the crime with a Ben Franklin impersonator, whose thinning gray hair and tiny spectacles were not for real. Both Mitch and Ben Franklin were nineteen. Ben Franklin had brought Mitch a hot dog and Coke from the nearest vendor.

"Thanks," said Mitch, eating the hot dog in two bites. He gave directions to Paul Revere's house and directions to the Aquarium and directions to Quincy Market and none of those lost people bought a T-shirt in exchange. Mitch remained cheerful.

"Drug deal," said Ben. "Who else drives limos? Plus the neighborhood's beautiful right here, but one block away, what have you got? Drug country. Filthy underpasses and shadowy caverns."

"Most of us call them alleys," teased Mitch.

Ben Franklin did not like being interrupted. "Who cares, I say? If drug dealers want to get rid of each other, that's fine, isn't it?"

Mitch and Ben Franklin began arguing the value of human life, if that life was scum and dreck.

The bricks were still blazing hot, and the sun was the same hazy gold. Its slanted rays blinded anybody without sunglasses.

An absolutely breathtakingly beautiful girl appeared.

She was drifting through the crowds as if walking through a watercolor. Or perhaps the girl herself had been painted on the landscape.

Mitch McKenna lost interest in the subject of crime.

Ben Franklin followed Mitch's eyes. "Wow," he agreed.

Wow was the only word for this girl. Just the kind of figure Mitch admired most, and thick full hair, which he loved. Mitch tried to catch her eye, but the girl didn't look his way. In fact, she didn't look at anything. Her hands were out in front of her, as if she were feeling in the dark. She acted like a blind person who'd lost her cane.

She had Wow-factor, all right. She was perfect. Mitch's pulse stepped up several beats.

His kid sister Ginger, who was not romantic, teased Mitch mercilessly because he was. He could hear her analysis even now. Love at first sight? his kid sister would shriek. Give me a break, Mitch. She's probably a schizophrenic shoplifter with nice hair.

Benches on which exhausted tourists could sink were everywhere and the girl made her way toward one. Her walk was too slow to be normal; her manner was confused. She wasn't stumbling — she remained graceful. But she saw nothing.

"There's a girl in need of a knight in shining armor," said Ben Franklin. "Shall I go discuss the Boston Tea Party with her?"

Mitch shook his head. "No. What she really needs is a good T-shirt."

They flipped a coin to see which of them got to be the friend this lovely girl so clearly required. Mitch didn't care what the coin said. He was going to be the friend if he had to weld Ben Franklin's glasses to the wagon.

Trembling, she carefully lowered herself onto a bench.

What a relief not to have to keep herself upright. Maybe now she could think clearly. Maybe it was the effort of walking that had prevented her mind from functioning. If only the solid smooth wood would hold her mind up as well as her body.

Her mind spun over nothing.

She was a leaf floating over open sea.

Her head ached terribly. Her skull, her eyes, and her brain all vibrated unpleasantly.

Her knees remained jelly. Her hands rested in her lap, as if stored there until needed. They were lovely hands; slim and competent, slightly curled as if ready to finger a violin. She wore no rings. On her wrists were no bracelets and no watch. There was no polish, clear or colored, on her gracefully shaped nails.

There was only one thing wrong.

One very major thing.

She did not know whose hands those were.

Her mind was empty. It had never happened to her before. She couldn't get past the blankness, or past the fear she felt because she had no mind.

Minds couldn't be empty! They were stuffed with facts and daydreams, thoughts and plans.

But her mind was empty.

There was something radically wrong. Something completely and totally off base. But she was too empty to know what it might be.

She focused on physical things. Swallowing. Breathing. Yes. She could do those. So why couldn't she also think?

She felt like a jar in a science experiment. Except she hadn't been used yet. She was just there on the shelf.

Her eyes were open. Her body was awake. But her personality slept.

It's one of those out-of-body experiences, she thought. The kind you hear about on weird TV shows: where the girl on the operating table finds herself in a pool of light up near the ceiling, listening to voices tell her it's not time to die.

I need a voice. Somebody tell me what to do. What am I sitting on this park bench for? For that matter, what park is this?

No answers floated forward. The emptiness continued on, as if she were filled, stuffed, overflowing! . . . with nothing at all.

I don't know my name, she thought.

She wrapped the five fingers of her right hand very neatly inside the five fingers of her left hand. They were very cold. But the day was hot. Summer day and winter hands.

Of course you know your name, she said to herself. Everybody knows her name. What's your name?

The hot wind crawled through her hair. The sun slanted into her eyes.

I don't know my name.

Chapter 2

I must know my name. People always know their names. So what's my name? Come on, don't get all worked up and silly, just think of your name!

She touched her throat.

No necklace.

No locket, no cross, no crystal, no delicate gold chains.

She wore no earrings. She touched her face and hair. The hair was long enough to pull forward and inspect. Deep rich brown, glinting with sun-dye. Like her hands, the hair seemed to belong to somebody else.

Okay. No clues there. Think about what's around you. Place yourself. You'll remember things once you see where you are.

She forced herself to focus her eyes.

Eyes. I don't know what color my own eyes

are. I'm not blind. I see. So why can't I also think and know?

Perhaps I'm participating in a very strange meditation rite, she thought. I'm pouring myself out onto the pavement. I'm evaporating in the sun.

She imagined herself baking into nothing, just as her mind felt baked into nothing. It was so scary she had to wrap her arms around herself to be sure she still had a body.

Come on. Think. Get a name. Get a fact. Pretend it's journalism. Who, what, where, why, when.

She could remember the five W's, but she could not answer a single one of them. She did not know who she was. Nor where she was. Nor why, nor when, nor what.

What is happening to me? Did I have a stroke? Is this heat prostration? Do I have amnesia?

A homeless man slouched toward her bench. As if she didn't have enough to worry about, now she had to wonder if he was safe, or if she should run.

Run? She thought. I can't even blink.

She risked a glance at the homeless person. He had the layers, the stumble, and the creepy eyes, but he wasn't filthy, his clothes weren't in shreds nor slept in, he carried no bags. He isn't homeless, she thought, he's a beggar, he's going to ask for money, and —

Yes! Of course! I have a handbag! That's why a fake homeless man is sidling up to me. He wants my money. Oh, thank you for letting me remember money. I'll look myself up in my wallet. My purse will get me launched again. Something happened to me here. I just need a clue, and I'll be fine.

She actually smiled. *Here you were thinking you had amnesia, or some crazy soap opera affliction like that. And all you have to do is —*

There was no purse.

Mitch won the coin toss, so Ben Franklin slipped inside the floorless wagon to hawk T-shirts for Mitch. Mitch adjusted his own T-shirt to look his muscular best.

Across the baking hot plaza, the lovely girl suddenly sat up, wild and panicky. She patted herself, looking between her feet — looking next to the bench — over the bench — looking here — there —

Purse panic. Women tourists always had immense handbags, since they were the family carrying case: sunglasses, Pampers, maps, just-purchased mugs, and postcards.

No need to rush, the purse was obviously long gone.

Mitch liked helping tourists. He had not yet had the opportunity to help a tourist as pretty as this. He hoped she would need lots of consolation. The closer he got, the more beautiful she looked — and the younger. He was two years into college, and he really didn't want to date a girl in high school. Boston had dozens of colleges, though. You wanted to study nursing or music, physics or piano repair, library science or computer engineering — this was the town. He hoped she would be a college girl.

People glanced his way, and he enjoyed that; he wanted to be visible. He did not seem to be visible to the girl, however. She was touching her extremities, like a space alien wondering what a nose or chin was for. On drugs? thought Mitch. Spaced out up to her lovely eyebrows?

She was truly lovely. Even though he was right next to her now, she still had that watercolor quality; a dreaminess around her edges. I'm in love, Ginger, Mitch silently told his sister. I don't care if she is a schizophrenic shoplifter.

Ginger could have told Mitch how Susan felt about him, and he would have been astonished. Mitch considered Susan his friend who happened to be a girl. The empty locket, however, he would have understood, because Mitch more or less had an empty locket of his own: in the little plastic sheaf that held credit cards and photographs in his wallet, he had saved a space. Someday he was going to have a girl's photograph there. Mitch had gone out with a lot of girls. Never with one whose picture he wanted in his wallet.

He had a clutching sensation in his chest, like a heart attack.

It *is* a heart attack, thought Mitch. It's a love-at-first-sight attack of the heart. He grinned. It was the kind of heart attack he'd been waiting for since he first discovered girls.

In his soothing, strangers-are-your-friend voice, he said to her, "What's the problem? May I help?"

How slowly she lifted her face to his, as if fighting gravity. When she finally focused her huge blurred eyes, she then actually set her hand on Mitch's chest, as if checking his heartbeat, making sure he was alive and not a store mannequin. It was okay with Mitch. He kept on grinning. Mitch had one of the world's better smiles, but the beautiful girl did not smile back.

"I — can't — find — my — purse," she said jaggedly, taking her hand back. Her voice shook. Her hands shook.

Poor kid probably had her plane ticket in there, her traveler's checks, the name and address of her motel. It was amazing how many people couldn't remember where they were staying. Mitch was always yelling for the beat policeman or telling tourists to call Travelers' Aid. He wasn't going to suggest Travelers' Aid for this girl. He would be all the aid she could require. "What's your name?" he said gently. He was dying to know her name. He needed her name. He had a weird superstitious feeling that once he said her name, he would link himself to her.

Since she was fighting tears, it took considerable effort for her to form an answer. It took Mitch considerable effort not to hug her. She just looked perfect for hugs. He wanted to touch her hair, which was absolutely gorgeous: bronze statue-in-a-museum brown: shining sunset-in-the-dark brown.

She touched his chest again, fingertips only, and stared, as if searching for his heart. Or hers. At last she spoke, in a husky close-to-tears voice that wrenched Mitch's heart. But what she had to say was impossible.

"I don't know my name," she whispered.

Mitch could just imagine what his sister Ginger would have to say about that.

He was having the funny feeling he'd seen this girl before. Mitch saw hundreds, maybe thousands, of people every day out here. They were all going on the Freedom Trail, hunting down Paul Revere's house and the Old North Church. Had he seen her as a tourist? A T-shirt buyer?

Or had he seen her on TV? She was lovely enough for television. And if that was where he'd seen her, then she was an actress, and this was an act.

But what would the act be for? Why fake memory loss? What could she hope to accomplish?

It must be real.

But was amnesia ever a real medical condition? Could you actually forget the name you'd been called all your life? Maybe if you got hit on the head. But she looked fine to him. Admit it, she looked world-class to him. If there was any skull damage, it was perfectly concealed by that perfect hair.

But, say she really couldn't remember her name. Say the amnesia was real. What should he do about it? Call an ambulance? He did not want a problem as attractive as this in anybody's hands but his own. On the other hand, if she had a concussion, she shouldn't be up and walking around. She should be in a hospital bed. Wouldn't it make it worse, to slosh her brains around instead of lying still?

Doesn't know her name, thought Mitch ruefully. Would Ginger ever cackle with laughter now. So much for falling in love across the crowded plaza.

Tourists, sick of Revolutionary War history and eager for entertainment, listened in. They were pretty sure it was a hoax. Maybe a movie being filmed. Or some cleverly staged con. But she was a real beauty. Hoax or not, she held the crowd's attention.

Word spread. Strangers gossiped as if they were old buddies in a coffee shop. Tourists from Japan asked tourists from Alabama exactly what was going on. People came out of the hotel to monitor the situation. People crowded around to hear better and some of them took photographs, in case this was going to be on national television.

"Amnesia?" said a stout woman leaning on a goose-head cane. "Don't you have to get whacked on the head? She doesn't seem hurt."

"You can get shocked enough to forget," said somebody else. "Maybe she had a terrible shock."

A tourist sympathetically bought the girl a lemonade. She closed her hands around the paper cup like an extraterrestrial who was unfamiliar with liquid.

In mid-afternoon, the restaurant where Susan Nevilleson waitressed was open, but business was very slow. She saw the crowd gathered around Mitch McKenna, and said to Michael, the headwaiter, "I'm going on break, Michael."

Michael peered out the door. "You mean, you're going to check out Mitch."

"That, too." Susan didn't peel off her apron. The restaurant required them to dress period style: Susan wore a dark blue cotton dress, floor length and ruffled, with an enormous white starched and bibbed apron. Tall girls looked quite wonderful. Susan, however, looked ready for the third-grade Thanksgiving play. She lifted her skirts in order to cross the plaza speedily. Nobody gave her a second glance. In Boston in the summer, you expected people to dress like colonial dames.

Susan was too small to break through the crowd and too small to see the attraction.

"Amnesia!" said a woman in the crowd. "Just like a soap opera."

"Does amnesia really happen?" said somebody skeptically.

"They wouldn't have amnesia on the soaps

if it didn't happen in real life," said somebody else with assurance.

Susan was irritated. She felt women should have better things to do in life than watch television weekday afternoons. "Nothing in a soap opera has anything to do with real life," said Susan, and she shoved hard and broke through the press.

There was Mitch, the love of her life, holding the two hands of an utterly impossibly beautiful girl, a girl who was everything Susan was not: tall, slender, tan, athletic, stunning . . . and needy. The girl was trembling, and Susan could tell that Mitch loved that. He, Mitch, T-Shirt God, would wrap his biceps around her and carry her off to safety.

Mitch's horizons had just narrowed. There was nothing in Mitch's world except this girl, and her soft skin, and her bronze hair, and her frightened eyes, and her open lips.

I hate her, thought Susan.

Mitch was quite astonished when Susan suddenly appeared next to him, like a kid at a library story hour. He felt trespassed upon. This was *his* Miss Amnesia. He didn't want to share her with Susan.

Susan said, "Amnesia? Come on. *Amnesia*?"

She made it sound like a rare tropical disease that only three people on the planet had ever suffered, and none of them were from Boston.

Mitch would have glared at Susan but he was afraid Miss Amnesia would think he was glaring at her. She was beyond teasing. Susan shouldn't do it. He tried to look comforting and safe. When the girl lifted her dark eyes to his, Mitch was shocked. The girl was terrified. She was a cornered animal. Not only afraid, but afraid of *him.*

The amnesia is for real, thought Mitch. She's as afraid of us as if we were armed against her. We might as well be. We know who we are. She doesn't.

He could not imagine the eeriness of it. To go on standing and breathing and being alive — but not know who you are.

He wanted to wrap his arms around her, protect her from the fear that shivered through her like fever. He had always kept his distance from needy girls. Now the last thing he wanted was distance.

Susan, in her rather piercing voice, the one she used in drama class to reach the back row, said, "Bet I can guess your name. I know all the popular names. Let's see. You're — Jessica?"

The girl focused on Susan, her eyes growing wider and wider, taking in so much sunlight it would blind her. Breathing hard enough to faint.

"Jennie?" said Susan. "Kara? Kristin? Ashley?"

In the heat multiplied by stones and bodies, the girl shivered. She closed her eyes, as if to close out the sound and sight of Susan.

The crowd began to offer names, too. "Megan? Heather? Kelly? Emily?" they said, going for the popular.

The girl clung to the paper cup of lemonade as if it were all she had. In fact, it *was* all she had. No purse, no backpack, nothing in her pockets.

The girl shook her head. Her hair fascinated Susan. It was very thick, and multicolored, but it was not dyed. Susan knew these things. The heavy hair stayed put, as if it were made of some other material altogether than Susan's baby-fine locks. Her lips moved, and Susan could lip-read "I don't know," but fear had drained off sound. It wasn't even a whisper.

Mitch didn't even care now whether the girl was in high school or college. Anything she was would be perfect. He just wanted to help her, to jostle her mind, find the key to open her thoughts. He moved on to location. "Do you know where you are? This is Boston."

The girl seemed truly astonished, even horrified, by that information. Mouth open, lips trembling, brows drawn, she stared beyond the crowd toward the water, and then swung around to look at the impenetrable walls of the buildings behind her. *"This is Boston?"* she cried.

Where did you think it was? thought Susan irritably. Moscow?

The girl grew so pale that Mitch obviously felt the only decent thing to do was put his arm around her. The crowd — excepting Susan — sighed happily. They hoped she would rest her head against him, and they would actually witness love at first sight, but she simply was rigid and frightened, more imprisoned than comforted.

Susan's hair prickled. What girl would refuse a hug from Mitch?

Only a girl too panicked to see him clearly. Could this girl actually have amnesia? Susan had written her off as a sicko wanting attention. But if that were the case, the girl would certainly accept Mitch's attention. That would be the whole point: attention.

Susan studied the girl more carefully. She

was so lovely that even Susan had seen nothing but face and figure. Now she saw expensive but casual clothes, and absolutely nothing in the way of possessions. There were pockets in the long shorts, but nothing in them. No shirt pocket. No purse. No jewelry. No nothing.

You did not travel in a city without something. You had to have a wallet. You had to have money, or car keys, or commuter tokens. Even if you lived nearby (especially if you lived nearby; away from the tourist-attracting wharves, this could be a dangerous part of the city) you had to bring your door key. You couldn't leave your door unlocked and go for a stroll.

Where had she come from?

Had somebody robbed her?

But the girl looked fine. No bruises. No torn clothing. No lumps on the head. No bleeding.

She's an actress, thought Susan. But then, since I want to be an actress, and Mitch and Ben want to be actors, and we would be drama majors if our parents weren't insisting on more intelligent lines of study, I always think in terms of acting. Most people aren't on their own personal stage. And if it's an act, who is this girl's audience? She couldn't care about tourists, could she? And she clearly doesn't care about handsome young men, or she'd be in Mitch's arms right now.

The actress in Susan tried to lose her memory, her name, her life, her past. It was horrible to imagine standing in a strange place among strange people *and knowing absolutely nothing.*

Because his T-shirt was too small for him, Susan actually saw Mitch's lungs working harder.

Of course he's going to fall in love with her, thought Susan, her own heart aching. A mysterious beautiful girl without a name? It's Mitch. This is the scene he wants to play.

Mitch was as lost to Susan as the beautiful girl's memory was lost. The hostility and anger Susan expected to feel drained away. She felt incredibly tired and used up.

Oh, Mitch. I wanted you so much, and you never knew.

The tourists pressed up against the girl.

She was sick, her stomach and throat betraying her. She got nausea just from their eyes, their greedy interest, even their laughter. Some of them thought it was funny.

People snapped pictures of her, as if she were a display in an historic building.

The small woman in the long, old-fashioned clothing kept throwing names at her, like darts. Trying to pierce her thinking with the right name: Kelly, Megan, Sarah, Jill.

Would I know if she said the right name? Or would it just be a syllable in a list?

Funny, she thought desperately. Maybe I should just pick one of her names. Choose a syllable, pretend I'm fine, get out of here.

And go where?

Where do I live, where is my house, who is my family, *what is my name?*

"Forgot her name?" said somebody skeptically. "Right. Tell me another one."

Laughter.

"This is a stunt. It's for some TV show to find out how gullible the public is. See if we fall for this or not."

It was too much. Her eyes overflowed. She reached for a Kleenex, but of course she didn't have one — she didn't have anything — and her rescuer silently handed over his handkerchief. Actually, it was a bandanna. Bright red with black patterns. It relaxed her, and he smiled into her smile. For a tiny moment, the trouble she had breathing had nothing to do with memory loss.

He was beautiful, in that rare masculine way. Not handsome but beautiful. Perfect.

She had not bargained for this. Somebody so attractive she wanted to forget everything else.

But I have forgotten everything else, she thought.

Chapter 3

Mitch kept expecting cops to show up, but maybe they were sick of this corner of the world. After all, they'd spent hours talking to people about a thirty-second drive-by shooting, which was probably a drug deal, or a really angry rich couple having a really hard time dividing the money in the divorce. Why come back for a teenage girl who doesn't know if she's Molly or Katie?

But the man who strode through the crowd was no cop. Tall and thin, he looked like a secretary of state whose life was bound up in difficult, consuming situations. He had deals to make. Diplomacy to factor in. Conference calls to get back to. His white collar was buttoned down, and his cuffs were held by links, not buttons. His tie was dark crimson with navy stripes, an alma mater tie; a tie to show how distinguished he was.

"What is going on here?" said the man quietly. His diction matched his suit: sharp and creased.

Mitch was still holding the girl, however lightly. He felt her shivers right through the lines in his palms. He might have been reading her future. She was still terrified. "The young lady," said Mitch carefully, "does not seem to remember her name, nor where she lives."

The man simply stared at Mitch. His composure was shaken. When he'd finished staring at Mitch, he stared at the girl. "Hope, what is he talking about?"

Although Mitch was delighted that a distinguished personage like this man had something to do with his beautiful watercolor girl, he was sick with disappointment that his moment as Travelers' Aid was over. He had wanted her to stay Unknown. A Mystery.

Nice guy, he said to himself. Damsel in distress gets identified and you'd rather have her sobbing.

But she had not sobbed. She had hung onto herself, been pretty classy about it, in fact. Just as the name Hope was pretty classy. Hope. He liked that. "Hope," he said to her softly.

Hope herself said nothing. She did not look less afraid. If anything, her anxiety moved toward terror. She began to breathe far too quickly, as if she would take in too much oxygen, and collapse in some sort of reverse faint.

What would I have done with her? wondered Mitch. Taken her home with me? Bought her dinner on the theory that calories restore memories?

Hope, thought Susan Nevilleson. What a classy name. It suits her. And they look alike, that man and her. They're both so long and lean and *rich* looking.

The girl swept that bronze statue hair off her face, hanging onto the hair, as if to a lifeline, and then blinked her beautiful eyes. She said nothing, but just pitifully shook her head.

The man regarded the girl soberly. "This is my daughter," he said to Mitch. He sounded very tired, as if he were past his limit. Mitch was struck by how few gestures he used: he didn't rub his eyes or shake his head or press his lips together.

A sigh ran through the crowd.

His daughter. Too bad. No film, no stunt, no nothing. She'd been identified too easily. Amnesia was so much more fun.

"Come, Hope," said her father. "We'll go inside and work this out." He took his daughter's arm, but she jerked free. Smothering a cry, Hope stepped quickly back, pressing against Mitch's broad chest. She rubbed her bare arm where her father had touched her, eyes wide with fright, unable to come up with speech any more than she had been able to come up with her name.

The tourists reacted. They were ready to save the girl. If this guy was mean to her . . . if she had reason to be scared of him . . .

Trembling, the girl ran a hand down her own throat, arching and tightening the fingers as if describing herself in sign language. "I don't know what's happened," she said. "I don't know if I was hit on the head or if I've had too much sun, or what could have gone wrong, and if you're my father, I'm sorry, but I don't remember you."

Only then did the father become aware of the fascinated crowd. He controlled his features, which had been extremely controlled already. "Hope, this is going too far. I suppose I can endure this. I've endured everything else you've done. But why must you do this kind of thing to me, Hope? In public, no less?"

The girl shivered. It was a completely genuine shiver.

Her father was not moved. "Hope, I don't know what you're up to this time, but you may talk it over with your psychiatrist on Monday. You have wasted my entire afternoon with your antics. We have been searching for you for hours! And here you are, right outside the door."

The door? The only door they were outside of was The Jayquith. Some of those suites took entire floors and had their own elevators. Supposedly they charged a thousand dollars for one night in their best suite!

Mitch, who stared at The Jayquith all day, stared again. A magnificently garbed doorman stood inside in the air-conditioning, arms folded. He was removed in every way from tourist troubles on the pavement, a sort of proof that anybody who stayed at The Jayquith would be removed from any kind of trouble.

The girl said, "But I don't know you. How can I go somewhere with a man I don't know?" She clung to Mitch's arm without seeing Mitch.

But this appeared to be a script her father had heard before, and would hear again, and furthermore had to pay a psychiatrist to hear as well. Now he was being humiliated in front of a crowd of camera-toting strangers.

Susan could feel the father's loathing of the publicness of this. How he despised being watched, being entertainment for the crowd!

He managed to not actually look at anyone, and yet he controlled them, as a fine actor controls his audience. "My daughter is making a scene," he said quietly, but like a stage actor, his voice carried neatly to the last person in the crowd. "I thank all of you for showing concern. It makes me proud to be a Bostonian. However, I'm sorry to say my daughter is just a spoiled debutante who cannot bear a day without attention. Although," and here his voice cracked, "I did not expect her to come down and put on an amnesia display."

The crowd's heart shifted to the father. Imagine being the parent of such a rotten kid. Obviously she could make the choice to be nice. Instead she was subjecting her father to public humiliation. You thought wealth and beauty were everything, but then you saw something like this.

Susan was a little shocked. Faking amnesia to get some twisted revenge on her family? That was really sick. What kind of nasty little family did these people have behind those magnificent doors? Even Mitch blinked.

Good, thought Susan, he'll fall out of love with her now.

"Where's your purse, Hope?" said her father.

Hope shook her head confusedly.

"She lost it," Mitch told him.

"How do you know?" asked the father.

"She told me so."

The father tightened his lips. It was clear that his daughter said a lot of things that weren't true.

"I'm Mitch McKenna," said Mitch, sticking out his hand for the father to shake. Susan knew what was going on; Mitch wanted their phone number. The father shook Mitch's hand once, hard, like an engine piston, and let go.

"If I had my purse," said Hope, "I'd take out my license and I'd know who I am and where I live."

"You live," said the father, "at The Jayquith. Let's go in so you can lie down, and I'll call your doctor."

She *lived* at The Jayquith? That was impressive enough.

The crowd studied Hope and her father. Yes. These were people who would have their own elevator, their own suite, and their own psychiatrist making house calls.

I knew it, thought Susan. She does have everything: wealth, looks, mystery, family. Of course, she's a nutcase.

Susan watched Mitch watching Hope.

Mitch himself felt almost drowned by Hope's presence. And very aware that she had not reacted as if the name Hope were familiar. Of course, if she really had amnesia, she didn't know the name. And yet, no matter how your memory failed you, could you fail to know your own father? Surely, even if words were gone, and facts were gone, she would know his face, his body, his presence.

But she didn't.

The man had to be her father. Who else on earth but your real parent would humiliate himself like this to claim you? Plus, he looked quite like his daughter. Tanned and athletic. Gray hair, of course, but the crispness of his suit certainly matched the crispness of her shirt.

Still, Mitch stayed between father and daughter, as if to take custody. There was something wrong with the level of her fear. He felt her preparing to run, and he could not decide what he would do if she chose that. Chase her? Bring her down and return her to this man?

Mitch could not make things add up.

He was as tall as the father and much, much stronger. He took a chest-expanding breath to demonstrate that little truth to Dad. He said, "I wonder if we could see some proof of that, sir."

The father stared at him. If he had been stunned to find his daughter was pretending to have amnesia, he was truly shocked when some hotshot musclebound college kid in a T-shirt demanded proof. He gave Mitch the look that adults give children who have stepped beyond the bounds of good behavior. "You've been extremely kind to my daughter," he said. He pivoted and led his daughter into the hotel. Hope went right along, as if this was the ending she had expected. She did not thank Mitch, and she did not look back.

Susan watched them go. The hotel personnel all but took the door off the hinges in their haste to please.

The crowd was satisfied. A girl as beautiful as that, it was only right that she should be rich enough to stay at The Jayquith. This was just the right father for her, too: distinguished and worldly. And, of course, she had a shrink. These super-rich kids, they knew their shrinks better than their mothers.

It was getting late, and people were tired. The crowd broke up to consider important things, like which restaurant would be the best end to a long day.

Susan wondered if maybe Michael would fire her for taking too much of a break. She would love to be fired. There had to be a better way to earn a dollar. Why hadn't she been born to

Jayquith Hotel money? She returned slowly to work.

Mitch knew exactly what his sister Ginger would say about Hope's character, and family, and how he should scrupulously avoid them.

Mitch, however, could have lifted Hope's footprints off the pavement and bottled her scent from the air. Hope, he thought. I love that name. It's perfect. It's the name I've been waiting for.

All I need now is the last name to go with it.

And the phone number of course.

Not to mention the first date.

Hope could feel the man's humiliation. She could almost feel the history of their relationship: how she always hurt him, and he somehow went on being a loving father anyway. It shamed her to look upon his face, and see that tired endurance. She must have put those lines there. She must be responsible for those gray streaks.

What she could not feel was any sense of familiarity.

Hope? she thought. I am a spoiled brat debutante? A daughter who makes absurd pathetic attempts to get attention? I am rich? I live in a hotel suite? In Boston?

She could get nothing out of it. She could connect nothing to it.

She was having such trouble breathing now she was all but shoveling air into her lungs.

Mitch had been watching her every reaction. She felt kinship with him; felt she'd known Mitch far longer than this man so politely escorting her away.

Right. Fifteen minutes longer.

I don't have to go, she thought. I can say no. I can walk away. I can hold onto this Mitch McKenna and wait the father out.

She tried to separate things: find common sense, find logic. But too much was happening and neither common sense nor logic came to mind.

She went with the man in the light gray suit into whatever world Hope occupied.

"I don't believe it," said Susan Nevilleson, who actually did believe it. "Amnesia. Piffle."

"You never believe anything," Mitch pointed out. "You're the most skeptical person I know." Mitch was mostly thinking about what he *could* identify: the husky, close-to-tears voice that made him want to hug that gorgeous girl again. The hug he had given but, also, the hug which Hope hadn't returned. He wanted her to return his hug. He wanted to feel the pressure of her against him, a two-way hug, the best hug. And that extraordinary hair, dark but sunny, that he wanted to twine between his fingers and brush across his lips.

Mitch remembered Ginger, which brought him down to earth somewhat. *You love hair that much, Mitch, quit Harvard and go to hairdressing school.*

Susan, staring out the restaurant window, pretended to wait at Ben Franklin and Mitch McKenna's table for some detailed special order. Flags whipped on tall poles. The final harbor tour boat was returning, and hundreds of passengers lined the immense bow. A reception had begun on the wedding-for-hire boat, and the bridesmaids, wearing a yellow so bright that Susan thought the guests should be handed sunglasses, were lining up for photographs. A Friday afternoon wedding. Susan wanted to marry Mitch, and she wanted a Saturday evening wedding. It seemed wiser not to discuss this with Mitch right now.

The little commuter boat, which took businessmen to their homes across the water, rocked as the passengers trooped steadily aboard. Beyond these, down a steep wooden connector, and across a narrow wooden dock, a magnificent private motor yacht was tied up. The *Lady Hope.* Her paint was a vivid indigo blue, and she gleamed as if, over the paint, she wore many coats of clear nail polish. Susan felt that she herself had great yacht potential. She tried to imagine having enough money to possess a boat like that.

Not that it was a *boat* Susan wanted to possess. She turned her attention back to Mitch. "If you're so worried," said Susan, "you should storm The Jayquith. Demand to see her."

Ben Franklin was confused. "Why should he do that, Susan?" Ben Franklin's real name was Rusty Corder, the first name a leftover elementary school joke. All his college friends had adopted his summer job name. Even though he had long since put away his rimless glasses, and neatly hung his wig on a hook, he was still Ben Franklin.

"Because Mitch doesn't think she knew the man," said Susan. "And the father refused to provide proof. Therefore she's being kidnapped."

Ben Franklin was exasperated. "Mitch, there's a lot missing from your plot. Why should the guy have to prove anything to you? And besides, why would you kidnap a person you don't know?"

"Either," said Susan, who often answered questions directed to other people, "because *you do* know who she is, and she's rich and is worth a fabulous ransom, or because *it doesn't matter* who she is. You have evil plans for her no matter what." Susan smiled gladly.

It seemed to Ben Franklin that you shouldn't be so happy at the idea of evil plans for that girl no matter what. "I'm not sure how easy it would be to get past the front desk at The Jayquith, anyway," he said. "That's why movie and rock stars go there. Because groupies can't penetrate the security." Ben Franklin watched Susan, whom he adored. Of course, she had to go and adore a stud. Namely Mitch. Mitch was flawless: every muscle developed; all profiles perfect; always tanned and never burned. His haircuts looked good even the first day. His eyesight was 20/20 and his voice was a beautiful tenor.

Plus Mitch was rich. Oh, he pretended not to be. He was clandestine about his wealth. The budget-conscious schoolboy. Please. Everybody knew who had wealth, and Mitch was known. He persisted in thinking that he had pulled off his poverty act.

Susan, of course, was just as drawn to Mitch's family money as she was to his body and soul.

Ben felt tired. He wasn't amazingly brilliant, he wasn't terrifically handsome, he wasn't awesomely rich. He wasn't a world-class athlete nor a world-burner in some fascinating subject. He was just solid. In all too many ways.

He was the only one of them who had actually gotten an acting job this summer, but it wasn't that great. He didn't want to be remembered as Ben Franklin. Okay, so Rusty Corder was a dumb name. But it was him, and he wanted people to like him, not his stage self. Especially Susan. He loved how small she was. How cute.

Nevertheless, he said out loud, cutting himself off at the knees, "What exactly would make you bother with Miss Amnesia at all, Mitch?" said Ben. "I mean, aside from the fact that she is physically perfect and unbelievably gorgeous."

"I'm in love with her," said Mitch.

Susan wanted to cry. Men. Boys. Ugh.

I can't bear it, she thought. He's falling head over heels in love with somebody else while I'm right here next to him. "Life isn't a chapter out of a storybook," she yelled at Mitch. "You can't just pick a girl off the sidewalk because she's beautiful, and decide this is your eternal romance."

"Sure you can. My father did."

Mitch was the only person Susan knew whose parents were perfect. Mitch had no my-childhood-was-rotten stories. Mitch had no my-parents-always-fought stories. Mitch had no you'll-never-catch-me-getting-married stories.

"Don't tell me about your father," said Susan testily.

But of course Mitch told her about his father.

"Parents are boring!" Susan grumbled. "Talk about us."

Mitch grinned. There was no "us."

"It's Friday night," Susan observed gloomily, wishing that tonight, after the restaurant closed, she and Mitch would become an Us. She turned her face away from Ben Franklin, who was gearing up to ask her out again. Couldn't he see that she had standards? And he didn't reach them?

Ben Franklin never kept up. Even in drama class, Ben had to have things explained to him over and over, in infuriating detail. Most people in drama class fantasized about beating Ben up even more often than they fantasized about being great actors. Susan wasn't going out with Ben.

Mitch picked up on none of this. He stared across the darkening square at the *Lady Hope*. The girl with the similar name floated lightly in the sea of his mind.

* * *

Every surface of The Jayquith gleamed. Jet-black marble graced the floor. Silver pearl papered the walls. The dark sofas in the lobby were glitter-woven with metallic threads. Forests of dark ferns filled immense baskets of moss. It was remote and cold. It was a place where no one would gather to chat. Laughter would not ring, and giddiness would be out of place.

Lobby hardly seemed the word. It was more like the elegant waiting rooms of palaces. Nor did hotel guests sit on the luxurious sofas. They strode through as if they never sat. Their lives too busy for mere sitting.

Dreamy French piano music was played by a half-hidden musician, whose sleek black dinner jacket perfectly matched his black concert grand.

It was music to be rich by.

The girl with amnesia needed a different kind of music. Music to match her heart, which was going crazy trying to pump enough energy into her system. Music to match her thoughts, which were crashing like lightning from sky to earth.

She felt surrounded by an army. All these uniformed people might have been employees of this strange man, and she might have been taken prisoner. As if this were no hotel at all, and never took guests, but merely pretended to do so.

Yet the man patted her shoulder easily and gently; he had done it a thousand times before; he was just a father comforting his daughter. "Sweetie," he said, "I never know what's going on with you, but I do know this. We've fumbled our way through a lot of scenes, and now we're going to fumble through this one."

They were not fumbling. They were moving as speedily as marathoners. Or was it her failing heart that made this seem so demanding? Perhaps along with everything else that had slipped out of focus, even her walk was receding.

"Now, Hope," he said softly, "it's going to be all right."

They were passing through reception rooms like swifts heading south. Before them lay the double doors of three elevators.

I cannot get into an elevator and enter a hotel room with someone I've never seen before in my life, Hope thought.

Yet the man was a father. She could feel him being a father. The kind of father every girl wanted: strong and firm, kind and understanding.

But I don't know him.

"I think I see what has happened," he went on.

A glittering hotel employee, dressed like a British soldier on the wrong side of the ocean, stood by the elevators. Two of those elevators could be opened by pressing UP or DOWN buttons. The third elevator required a key. The man smiled at them. "Good evening, sir." He bowed slightly to Hope.

Do you recognize me? thought Hope. Do I live here?

Hope's escort paid not the slightest attention to the elevator attendant. The man could have been an urn of lilies for all the response he got.

"You went out shopping," the father reminded her. "You wanted that new handbag. Remember? You left about noon."

It was true; she could remember a moment of wanting a new handbag. She tried to hang onto that moment, as she tried to hang onto her feet. Stop at the edge of this elevator, she said to herself. Don't cross that crack.

"I think you saw that terrible event in front of the hotel. That most unfortunate woman. We live in dreadful times. Considering the past and your nightmares, Hope, you have every right to be so deeply shocked. But I think we can work it through."

What unfortunate woman? What past? Work through to what? Who are you?

And over and over again, like a drum roll, she thought, *Who am I? Who am I? Who am I?*

The elevator doors opened. Inside, the cubicle was lined with gaudy red and gold paper that seemed to have nothing to do with the dark sophisticated elegance of the hotel. It was like a circus, a totally wrong place, a clue if she had ever seen one that she, too, was in a totally wrong place.

She could have refused to go with the man. She could have thrown herself down on the floor, yelled for the police. Could have screamed, *I don't know this man!* She even looked down at the floor to decide. The black marble was like sky in a thunderstorm, and the white veins in it, circles of lightning.

But she did nothing. Perhaps it was the elegant shimmer surrounding them; the quick pace of the guests; the urgent errands of the staff. Scenes did not belong in The Jayquith.

Or perhaps it was momentum. The thing had a speed of its own.

She thought of the rules for situations in

which you sensed trouble: scream, kick, run. Give them your money, give them your jewels. Never, never, let yourself be taken hostage.

Am I about to become a hostage?

Or a daughter in need of a shrink?

Chapter 4

"Go on, Mitch," said Susan. "Take a chance! Live dangerously! Storm The Jayquith!" Why am I encouraging him? she thought. The last thing I want is for Mitch to see more of Miss Amnesia. "Demand proof!" she went on giddily. "If they feed you to the sharks, we'll throw you a life preserver."

Because it's so dramatic, she thought. I love the stage so much, I'm willing to do anything for drama, even if it's the end of my hopes.

The end of her hopes would be Hope. Perhaps there was a poem in that, or rock lyrics, and she could make a fortune by —

"They don't call them life preservers anymore," said Ben, who was no poet, "because they often fail to preserve life. They just keep your chin above water if you're lucky. Now they're *throwable personal flotation devices.*"

"Cute," said Susan.

"I believe," said Mitch, "that Hope needs a throwable flotation device right now. Namely me." He flexed his shoulders in anticipation.

Ben laughed at him. "She already got rescued by a billionaire, Mitch," Ben pointed out. "The guy has a suite at The Jayquith. She's going to leave with a nineteen-year-old T-shirt seller? And what if she does come with you? Is somebody here planning to adopt her?"

"You're looking too far ahead," said Mitch. "I'm just entertaining myself on a slow Friday night in July. The beach is too far away and Paul Revere's house is closed." Mitch was beginning to get an idea: a stage scene, complete with dialogue.

Michael, the headwaiter, mentioned that it would be nice if Susan paid attention to her other tables. Nobody paid any more attention to Michael than Susan paid to her tables.

"Mitch, Miss Amnesia went into The Jayquith without screaming," said Ben Franklin. "You saw her. She doesn't want to be rescued. Her father doesn't want her to be rescued."

"And do we have proof that he's her father?" demanded Mitch. Suppose, he thought, that I confronted the father and said that *somebody else* had been looking for this same girl! Then he'd have to prove to me that he's her father, wouldn't he?

"No," said Ben Franklin, "but the man's had a long day. Whatever is going on, I don't see him being very welcoming to some college kid who wants to practice his drama club improvisation class."

Mitch loved improv. It was scary, up on stage with strangers, not a minute to think about what to do, just winging it, making up the lines as you went, responding to whatever the others said. When he was on stage, he truly lived his part. He wasn't Mitch McKenna, whoever that was. He was his role.

I know, thought Mitch, figuring out his skit. I'll say that some handsome college guy has been asking people if they've seen his girlfriend, who didn't show up for a date she would never have missed. I'll say he had a photograph of her. I'll say it sure looked like the very same person who was just claimed as his daughter. I'll need a name. What name shall I give this supposedly missing girlfriend supposedly searched for by this supposed boyfriend?

Mitch stood up. Six-two. Hundred and eighty. He took a deep breath and the T-shirt stretched. Susan giggled. "The Improv God," she told him. Mitch bowed, in complete agreement. I'll name my nonexistent missing girlfriend Susan, he decided. Easy to remember.

Ben Franklin said, "Don't, Mitch. There's something wrong with the picture. You don't wanna be in it."

Mitch grinned. The grin was so wide, so delighted, so masculine, that Susan blinked back tears.

"I do want to be in Hope's picture," Mitch said. He got up from the table, handing Susan to her headwaiter, and the check to Ben Franklin. "Pardon me," he said. "I have a hotel to crash."

They entered the elevator, just the two of them, and fluidly it moved upward. She pressed back against the inside wall and the velvety flocked circus paper was soft against her bare skin.

But the father only sighed. Facing the closed doors, patiently waiting to reach their floor, he said tiredly, "You need dinner, Hope. You're light-headed."

What a perfect description. She actually felt as if her skull had lost weight, ceased to be bone, was light and wind, and floating away from her.

They got off at the seventh floor.

Nothing — not one thing — was familiar to Hope.

The door was held for her, and she walked into the suite in The Jayquith.

Oh, but it was beautiful! You didn't need a memory to appreciate such beauty. An immense living room sparkled as if with precious stones. Pearl, ruby, and amethyst. Huge windows were the perfect height above the wonderful harbor view.

The room floated, like a magic carpet.

She was awestruck . . . and a stranger.

Yet splendid as the room was, it was definitely a hotel room. Luxuriant drapes, deeply stuffed sofas, gleaming cherry furniture, perfect symmetry, flawless condition . . . and not a single personal possession.

The green marble of the low table between the sofas looked, on second glance, like an unchiselled tombstone.

Not a magazine, not a pair of earrings, not a souvenir, not a sculpture, not a half-finished glass of water, touched any surface.

Perhaps the maids had just finished in here, or perhaps the occupants owned nothing; just as she had stood in that square with nothing at all in her hands or pockets.

Perhaps when you were as rich as this,

when you owned floors in hotels, perhaps you didn't also own clutter and mess.

The father lowered himself onto a sofa and regarded her silently. A Rolex watch gleamed on his right wrist and a thick gold wedding band circled his left ring finger.

He made no suggestions to her. The silence was large and she fought a desire to fill it either with babble or screaming.

He just looked at her. There was no expression on his face. He seemed comfortable — with her, with The Jayquith, with memory loss.

She was hideously afraid. It was almost impossible to fill her lungs now. She had not known that breathing could turn into a fight. Fear could make your own lungs the enemy. Her breath came in little shallow grabs for air.

She needed to sit or she'd topple over. She chose an immense forest-green leather sofa opposite him. The sofa was the most comfortable luxuriant couch on which she'd ever relaxed. It welcomed her like favorite pillows. Like soft night. "I didn't know leather could be colored," she said.

He said nothing.

What is memory, she wondered, that so much could be disposed of? So little kept?

What do I know of memory? But then, what does anybody know of memory? It keeps its own secrets, it has its own rules.

He's wearing a ring, so he's married. To my mother? If he's my father, I have a mother. Well, of course I have a mother. All human beings have mothers.

Hope was so confused that it seemed she wasn't really thinking, but just reading about somebody else's thoughts.

"Tell me what happened, Hope." His voice was calm, and rather sad.

She was suddenly deeply embarrassed. She had no idea what to do next. To say out loud yet again — *I don't know who you are. I don't know who I am, either* — it was too dumb. She just wanted this to end. He was such a nice man. He was being so kind. The whole thing was so weird. "Look," she said, and she had to put a hand over her mouth to keep herself from crying, which was odd, because tears didn't come from the mouth, "look, I'm truly sorry, but I — um —"

The father shook his head. "I half believe you, Hope," he said. "But it's hard to believe more than half. How could you really forget who you are? Now look." He meant that literally, for he got up, crossed the room, sat beside her, took her face and turned it up to his. His hands were as calm as his voice. His eyes were affectionate and understanding.

She began to cry.

"Tell me, Hope."

"I can't stay with you. I don't know who you are. I know you mean well, but I —" She still had Mitch McKenna's bandanna. She clung to it. It smelled of nothing, as if it were nothing, as if she too were nothing.

"Is that yours?" said the father. It was easier thinking of him as *the* father instead of *her* father.

She shook her head. "Mitch gave it to me. The boy who was helping me in the plaza. I was crying then, too."

"There is nothing to cry about. You're home. You're with me. All we need to do is find out what set this off." He picked up a telephone and ordered dinner to be sent up from the hotel restaurant.

Dinnertime? she thought. Where did the day go? Where have I been all day? Through a huge strip of glass on the far wall, she could see the sun going down. I've lost the day, she thought.

The silence in the room was awful. She kept having to fill it. "This is very scary. I mean, I really can't think very clearly."

He simply looked exhausted. "Hope, do you realize what you're putting me through? What would your mother think of this?"

What *would* my mother think of this? she wondered.

"Hope, no more soap operas. No more stunts."

She tried to meet his skeptical gaze but got only as far as his chest. She had to drop her eyes. *I'm not pretending,* she reminded herself. *This is real.* "It isn't a stunt," she said at last. Her voice shivered over the syllables, and she pressed the bandanna to her face. Mitch had seemed so normal out there in the sun. But what if she had lost normalcy? What if this loss of memory and space never ended? What if she got trapped in this thing?

The father paced. How neat his steps were. How composed his manner. She liked him. She liked how nice he was being in spite of her.

His polished shoes on the dark wine and green of the carpeting made no sound. In fact, nothing in this suite made any sound. The absence of noice was complete. No machinery hummed, no appliances clicked, no footsteps rang. The suite felt entirely and forever empty, as if its bare rooms went on and on, its closets and lives as empty as the top of the coffee table.

She wanted to be back in that outdoor square, among the pointing tourists, smelling salt water and hamburgers, hearing seagulls and boats' horns. She wanted to flirt with Mitch instead of —

Okay, but I'm here. And it's time to go on.

"Would you please tell me your name?" she said.

Now he did glare at her. Not dangerously. It was the glare of a parent who has put up with enough nonsense and is going to get really angry if you push another inch.

Hope actually blushed, as if she had some nerve asking what his, and presumably her, last name was.

From a corridor she had not noticed suddenly sprinted a tall and very thin girl. The girl's arms waved like Dutch windmills. She had the body of a nine-year-old playing tag. Her face, however, was seventeen or eighteen. Her short light hair was cut like overlapping shingles on a roof. A pattern had been carved in the hair. A looping spiral of shaven scalp came to an arrow-tipped point at the top of her head. It was a curled, hissing, snake.

Hope rather liked the haircut. Incredibly dramatic. It would take such nerve to do that. Hope could not imagine requesting it.

The girl was not dressed punk. She was dressed like a young Sunday school child: pink lace and white collar. Her head just didn't match her clothing, any more than her arm-flinging dancing matched her age. She looked like a plastic doll with the wrong head stuck on.

The girl hurled herself on the father, kissing him and mussing his hair. Then she flung herself on top of Hope, whose cheek she pecked while laughing aloud. It was an odd, hot, breathy kiss.

She knows me, thought Hope. She knows me very well. But —

"Darling, tell me all about it. I don't believe Uncle Ken for a moment. Amnesia! Please. You can do better than that. You always have." She flopped onto the leather sofa right next to Hope.

Uncle Ken, thought Hope, saving the new fact.

But the snake-etched girl wasn't leaving her much time to contemplate names. "Is it true you saw the shooting, Hopey? How too exciting. Tell me everything."

Hope wet her lips and the girl imitated the action perfectly. Hope pressed her lips together and the girl did that also. Hope had to laugh. The girl said, "Hopester, you are sitting on the couch as if you think it's going to scrape your leg, like barnacles."

"I'm kind of nervous," said Hope.

"You're kind of nuts," said the girl. "I admit, I'm impressed. You've never pulled this much off before. But enough's enough, Hopey." She scrunched up, tiny pointed chin resting on skinny little fist. Her nine-year-old, scout-getting-a-badge eyes focused unblinking on Hope's.

"But who are you?" said Hope.

"Hope, I don't put up with you. You know that. I'm not going to cater to your scenes." The girl turned to her uncle. "Did I hear you order dinner? I want dessert first. I'm sick of always having to have the main course first."

"Fine," said her uncle.

"I need chocolate before anything else," the girl explained to Hope. "Come on, Hope. Fess up. Tell all. What happened? What did you see? No fair not sharing."

Hope shook her head slowly. "I have nothing to share," she said. "I know how dumb I sound. I know how annoyed you must be. But I don't know you. I don't know why I even came up here. I should have — "

"Okay, okay." The girl tucked her long thin legs up under her dress. "I'll play along. I'm your cousin Kaytha." She giggled. "You're my cousin Hope. Our last name is Senneth."

Senneth.

Hope Senneth. Ken Senneth. Kaytha Senneth.

Hope ran her mind over Boston names she knew. Paul Revere, John Hancock, Sam Adams, John Quincy Adams. The name Senneth meant absolutely nothing to her.

"We share tutors, Hopesy. We don't go to school. We cruise the world, bringing our teachers along. Now and then we go to international schools, if we stay in port long enough. You are a much much much much better student than I am."

"Don't go to school?" repeated Hope. "Cruise the world?" She was beyond thinking. Beyond planning. Beyond anything. "But — you'd have to have — you know — passports, and — I'd have to — you know —"

"Hopester, cut it out. You're being truly annoying."

Food arrived.

Splendidly uniformed staff brought immense silver trays, laden with lidded platters. They swooped in gracefully, setting the dining table in a flash. The dining room also faced the harbor, its colors not wine and green like the sitting area, but mauve and silver. It did not feel like a dining room in a house; it felt like a private corner of a magnificent restaurant.

The napkins were mauve with silver threads, and folded like fleur-de-lis. Flowers and crystal water pitchers appeared, and Hope found herself being escorted to the table, her chair held for her. I'm famished, she thought. She could barely wait for the others to be seated.

The staff left and Hope tore into her meal.

"Hopesy," said Kaytha, "you're not a sled dog after a race."

"Sorry," she said, and she really was. Where were her manners?

Then she thought: With all that is going on here, why am I worrying for one tenth of a second about *manners?* She knotted her fingers together to keep herself from grabbing two forks at once and an hysterical giggle bubbled up in her throat.

"Has she been like this all afternoon, Uncle Ken?" said Kaytha. Sure enough, Kaytha was having an immense complex chocolate dessert, with layers of cake and sauce and whippings and toppings. Dessert first, thought Hope, and she knew absolutely that she had grown up in a household where dessert was a reward for eating your broccoli.

Out the great expanse of window, the setting sun turned the harbor to molten gold, and the sails of incoming boats were bejeweled triangles.

The father ate very slowly and studiedly. "Don't make it worse for her, Kaytha."

"It isn't worse for *her,*" said Kaytha, "it's worse for *us.* I still say if you'd just swing her against a brick wall somewhere, she'd start behaving."

"I think we'll stay short of that solution," he said dryly. He turned to Hope. "The problem — if there is one — is that you must have witnessed the woman in the limousine."

"I'm sorry, but I can't remember witnessing my entire life, never mind a woman in a limousine," said Hope.

"Pass the rolls, please," said Kaytha, and Hope passed the rolls, which were in a silver, rather than a wicker, basket, lined by a cloth so pretty it might have been a scarf. How normal it all seemed — passing rolls, buttering them.

"Start by telling me what you did today, Hope," said her father.

Normalcy vanished quickly. Hysteria crept back. "I can't tell you anything. I don't remember anything. I don't know what happened today or any other day. I don't know what's going on. Please! If you're really my father, explain what's going on!"

"Do you want me to call Dr. Patel?"

"Who is Dr. Patel?" she said nervously.

"Your psychiatrist. Whom you have seen twice a week for three years."

She tried to haul this into her mind, but her head stayed heavy, and nothing traveled with her. "Why do I go see him?"

"Her," corrected Mr. Senneth reproachfully. "Dr. Patel is a woman. As you well know."

"I don't know anything!"

"*Hope. Stop this.*" It was a father's voice. A father who was sick and tired of all this nonsense.

Kaytha's eyes glittered like glass and silver. She traced the snake shaved on her skull with a long fingernail.

"That is the creepiest thing I have ever seen anybody do," said Hope.

Mr. Senneth suddenly laughed, shaking his head. "You're right about that, Hope."

Kaytha was defensive. "I like my snake. I like to feel him curling himself up there."

"That's sick," said Hope. "When did you get the haircut?"

"Hopesy, you were with me. You chickened out. You kept your old hair."

My old hair. My hair that I don't even know what it looks like. I don't even know what I look like.

They actually know me. They are used to me. What is going on?

She pushed away the plate of food, pressed the bandanna to her face, and wept.

Kaytha was fascinated.

An empty head. No past. No facts. No plans for the future either. No anything.

Do I believe this? she thought. Is there really such a thing as amnesia? But what's the point in pretending?

In the midst of cousinly teasing, Kaytha paid extremely close attention to Hope. Assessing, gauging, wondering. It was so very very strange.

If Kaytha were in that position — couldn't remember her name, or Uncle Ken, or Cousin Edie, or The Jayquith — and, if on top of that, she had lost all her possessions — what would she do?

Nothing would make Kaytha approach a policeman.

She thought about Mitch the T-shirt God,

wrapping his arms around Hope. Kaytha suppressed the jealousy that threatened. There was no time for jealousy. Well, actually, she thought, we have till Tuesday. There probably *is* time for jealousy. But I'm going to be mature. After all, Hope didn't hug him back. She just stood there. I saw that from the seventh-floor window.

I'm still going to have Mitch for myself. There *is* time for that.

She said, "I have things to do, Hopesy. I'll see you later. Now listen to me. You know how much you detest Dr. Patel. You know what electric shock feels like. So lighten up and talk to Uncle Ken."

"Electric shock?" repeated Hope, mouth dropping and skin whitening.

"Stop it, Kaytha," said the father sharply. "She's just being mean, Hope. You two don't get along particularly well, in case that's another thing you're not remembering."

Kaytha needed to get out of the suite fast. She could not keep this up. It was just too, too weird. Kaytha waved at her uncle, drew a snake on Hope's hair, and left the hotel.

Hope was not relieved when Kaytha left.

The empty feeling in the suite and in her heart returned. How large emptiness could be!

The man sat opposite her, calmly eating his dinner.

She sat not calmly at all, wrapping and unwrapping the bandanna around her cold fingers. Kaytha had eaten only the dessert. When she left, after the snake tracing, she'd rested her hand on the back of Hope's neck. Feather light and very cool. As if Hope's first guess had been right, and Kaytha was a plastic doll.

But without another girl there, Hope felt immensely more vulnerable. I should have asked if I could go with her, she thought. I wonder what she's doing tonight.

I'm sitting at dinner with a man I've never seen before in my life, who claims I'm his psycho daughter, and I'm wondering if I should have gone out on the town with a cousin I don't know, to have a good time in a city I've never visited?

I *am* psycho.

The sharp rat-a-tat-tat on the hotel room door startled them both.

They exchanged looks of shock as identical as if they really were father and daughter.

With some annoyance, Mr. Senneth went to the door. Whatever he saw through the peephole stunned him. Slowly, but unwillingly, he unlocked and opened the door.

The T-shirt God grinned.

Even though a good portion of her life seemed to be missing, Hope knew that she had never been so glad to see anybody in all that life. When she beamed at him, tension and fear left.

"Hey there, Hope," said Mitch, grinning a quite amazing grin. "Are you okay?"

I am now, she thought. He's so handsome! And so normal! How do you get that normal?

"How did you get up to this floor?" demanded Mr. Senneth.

Mitch grinned even wider and winked. "Supernatural powers."

"I would like a better explanation than that, young man. What employee permitted you entry? I will have them dismissed. You have to have a key to make the elevator stop at this floor."

Mitch nodded several times, grinning wider with each nod, as if something in him were wound up. It provoked Mr. Senneth as much as it delighted Hope. "My parents stay here sometimes," he said, with an offhand little shrug. "I got the key from Mother."

"Your parents?" repeated Mr. Senneth.

"Well, not in this suite, exactly. There are four on this floor, you know. Mother prefers the east corner. She likes sunrise more than sunset."

Hope pictured Mother. A stout woman with a large bosom. Mother would be horrifyingly rich and underwrite entire television shows. Probably nature programs about odd little white birds on remote islands off Scotland.

Hope giggled to herself.

Mr. Senneth was not amused. "You're a persistent young man. I have to admire that. Your name was — uh —"

"Mitch McKenna."

"I am unacquainted with your parents."

"That's okay," said Mitch, walking around Mr. Senneth to go over to Hope.

"I can only assume," said Mr. Senneth icily, "that you have ripped off that Harvard logo you wear, and do not actually attend that college, or you would, I hope, display better manners."

"I'm sorry, sir," said Mitch, without committing himself about being a real Harvard student. He could not take his eyes off Hope. She could feel the extent of his crush on her, his fascination with her, right across the room, like static electricity. She left the table and walked toward Mitch. She felt like a gymnast on a balance beam. There was only one place to set each nervous foot, and each step led straight to Mitch.

"I fell in love with Hope this afternoon," said

Mitch, "so I had to come up, and make sure she's okay."

Hope felt herself laughing. This was so romantic. The pleasure of his company put a smile on her face way beyond the amnesia. "You did?" She held out her hands.

"I did." He held out his, and they touched fingertips, and then palms, and then curled their hands together.

"Are you okay?" he said softly.

"I have no idea what I am." She was entranced by him, forgetting how much she had forgotten. She still had his bandanna. "Very confused, I guess."

He lifted his hand, as if to touch her hair, but didn't, as if it were too much for him, as if they would fuse.

Mr. Senneth stepped between them. "Although you find it amusing and meaningless, my daughter continues to claim amnesia. We have a psychiatrist coming. We have family problems to work out. We do not want an interloper, young man, no matter how romantic. All you are is another problem."

Mitch had the grace to flush. He wavered. For a moment, the little boy he used to be showed much more clearly than the young man he now was. To Mr. Senneth rather than to Hope, he said diffidently, "Actually, sir, I'm here to see if Hope will come with me to the Boston Pops Concert on Sunday."

A date, thought Hope. I have literally lost my mind, and a boy who met me a few hours ago is asking me on a date. Can you be in love with somebody you don't know?

"No," said Mr. Senneth. "She may not."

"Aw, come on," pleaded Mitch. "John Williams is going to do all his movie themes. *Star Wars. Jurassic Park. Indiana Jones.* She'll love it." He faced Hope again. "Won't you, Hope?" He beamed at her.

We're planning my social calendar. And what about tonight? Do I sleep here? Do I have a room here? Does Kaytha come home?

"She isn't well," said Mr. Senneth.

Mitch jumped right into that. "I'd be great therapy."

"Please just steer clear of my family," said Mr. Senneth. He looked ill.

"I'm in love, Mr. Senneth. Guys in love don't steer clear, they steer forward."

"I'd love to go, Mitch," she said shyly. She actually looked at the father, as if apologizing for defying him. "When is the concert? What day is today? What should I wear?"

Mitch laughed out loud. She loved his laugh! What a great laugh. That was the laugh of a man you could spend a life with, and certainly an evening. Then she thought: What do I mean — what should I wear? I have no clothes.

She found herself staring down the corridor from which Kaytha had emerged before dinner, wondering if she did have clothes. If there was a closet there, filled with the dresses of Hope Senneth. "This is so strange," she said to Mr. Senneth.

"I certainly agree with that." And suddenly, surprisingly, Mr. Senneth said, "This is Friday, Hope. Yes. You may go to the Pops Concert on Sunday. By then I feel sure we'll have this — nonsense — squared away."

"Oh, thank you!" cried Hope, as if he *were* her father, and she *did* need his permission.

She tried to hug Mitch, as she had not hugged him in the plaza, but Mitch held her off. She was upset. What did that mean?

"There's another problem we need to discuss." His voice was serious, almost grim. It was a completely different voice from the comfort he'd offered in the plaza and from his rhapsody a moment ago. She was chilled.

Mitch paused, as if figuring out how to be polite about this. "I'm also here because another individual was asking after her." Mitch nodded gently toward Hope.

"Another individual?" repeated Mr. Senneth.

Hope forgot romance. *Another person* was looking for her? But —

"This guy came by," explained Mitch. "He claimed that his girlfriend, Susan Nevilleson, was supposed to meet him this afternoon. But she didn't show up. The guy had a nice black and white photo and it sure looked like — well — your daughter, Hope."

The silence was even deeper. Not one of them seemed to breathe. She could either be Hope Senneth or Susan Nevilleson.

She certainly could not be both.

If she had felt light-headed before, she felt carbonated now. Bubbles could burst the lid of her brain.

Mitch's smile tightened until it was just something to do with his mouth. "I thought of telling him to call the police," said Mitch, "or telling him about you, but then I decided I didn't want to cause any more difficulties for Hope." He shrugged slightly. "Or Susan." Mitch set his jaw to one side and reset it where it belonged. "I'd like proof, Mr. Senneth. Proof that this is your daughter. You know. Driver's license. Credit cards. Something."

Chapter 5

Nobody moved.

Nobody spoke.

Then Mr. Senneth shook his head. He was irritated, nothing more. Swiftly he crossed the sprawling room to a small delicate desk on the far side. A vase of fresh flowers, JAYQUITH writing paper, and a little crystal bowl of wrapped candy adorned the surface. Opening a drawer, he removed a dark blue pamphlet with a bright gold seal on the front.

A passport, thought Hope. I've never actually seen one. He's taking out a passport — *and it must be mine.*

She felt as if she had been poured out of some little bowl of her own design into a huge swimming pool of somebody else's. Would she be able to swim in this? Or would she drown?

My passport? There is proof?

She found herself walking to Mr. Senneth's

side, needing to see that passport, needing to read those words, stare at that photograph. Mitch joined her. They were standing next to each other like a couple as Mr. Senneth opened it to the page with the photograph.

How she loved Mitch's scent. It was not from a bottle: it was work and dust and cotton and male. She wanted to kiss him. She controlled that and looked at the passport instead.

The passport was old and well-used. Hope Senneth, as Kaytha had said, traveled the globe. Her photograph was as uncomplimentary as a driver's license photo. The lovely dark-haired Hope Senneth looked thirty-five. Her mouth was open but not smiling, so she also looked infantile. She looked, in fact, like the kind of girl who had never quite outgrown giggling to herself in the street.

She looks . . . like me, thought Hope. *She —*

but —

then —

I am Hope Senneth!

Hope took a time-honored way out of the situation.

She fainted.

For Susan, the restaurant seemed to stay open forever. She could not imagine, this Friday night, that they would ever close. Tourists stormed the place as if there was only one destination on earth: her tables. Every tray was as heavy as a tombstone and every order as complex as calculus.

She ran, she rushed, she carried, she obeyed, she smiled, she smiled, she smiled.

My smile is dead, thought Susan. You use a smile too much, it dies on you. They'd better give me good tips to compensate for the death of my smile.

Michael the headwaiter said, "Susan, darling, I think a break is in order. Before you go insane and become homicidal and start shooting people from the mast of *Old Ironsides*."

"How tempting," said Susan, so Michael drew her outdoors for five minutes of fresh air.

"Really, Susan. You're not cut out to be a waitress. You think more about Mitch than about who ordered steak rare and who's ready for the check."

"I know, Michael. I'm hopelessly in love with Mitch. No. I will not use that word. Hope is in it. Mitch is in love with Hope, you know."

"Miss Amnesia?"

"The very same."

"Susan, why can't you just love Ben Franklin

back? Mitch is a lost cause and Ben Franklin is a nice guy."

"He is not lost," said Susan. She didn't even bother to respond to the part about Ben Franklin. "I'm not losing Mitch. I'm not."

In the darkness of early evening they stared out over the harbor. Lights twinkled on masts.

Suddenly, the weird, skinny-thin girl with the snake carved in her hair, the one who kept buying T's from Mitch and had twice had lunch in the restaurant, emerged from The Jayquith and darted across the nearly empty plaza. Only a few lovers on still-warm benches were scattered in the shadows now. And possibly muggers. Susan wouldn't have taken the risk.

Michael said, "I love her hair."

"Would you do that, Michael? Cut symbols in your scalp?"

"If I were brave enough."

"I'd never do it. I think it's incredibly creepy. And where is she going? Look at her! Running down the wharves. What's she going to do, hurl herself into the waves?"

They were momentarily concerned. But although there was urgency in the girl's pace, she knew where she was going. There was no pause in her running. She was comfortable on the swaying wooden docks, loaded with coiled rope and electrical outlets and gas cans. Sure-footed as a gazelle, she dashed out as far as the docks stretched, her little pink dress puffing out around her skinny body.

She ran up the portable steps to the high impressive deck of *Lady Hope* like an agile elementary school kid racing up the steps of a slide.

"That's her boat?" said Susan, astonished.

"She sure boarded easily enough. She's done it before."

"I wish I were that rich," said Susan. "I know I could adapt to living on a fabulous yacht. I wonder, if I boarded the *Lady Hope*, if they'd be nice about it and show me around, or if they'd call the police."

"There's something about that boat," said Michael soberly, "that makes me think they would never call the police."

Susan was thrilled. "What do you mean, Michael? I've watched that boat for the whole ten days it's been docked out there. It's perfectly dull."

"I think they smuggle," he said. Michael was middle-aged and paunchy and had never previously said a single interesting word.

"Smuggle what? This is wonderful! This is so exciting!" cried Susan. Waitressing wouldn't be so bad if Susan got to hang out with smugglers, or smuggler-stoppers. "Do you think it's gold? Or selling beautiful young girls into slavery in some exotic harem?"

"No," said Michael. "It's got to be drugs. Think about it. That's an oceangoing vessel. It can go thirty knots, which is very fast. Two hundred gallons an hour in two engines. It could meet a shipment from South America out in the Atlantic Ocean and quietly sail back to its little private marina and sell off the drugs."

Susan wondered for a moment how Michael knew so much about *Lady Hope*. Michael must be the kind of male who took one look at a vehicle or ship, and automatically knew all. Ben wouldn't know that stuff, she thought. I bet Mitch would.

"It's not at a private little marina," Susan objected. "It's in the middle of Boston within sight of the priciest hotel in America." It occurred to Susan that a beautiful young girl actually *had* just disappeared into The Jayquith. What if Miss Amnesia — no, that was ridiculous. Her name was Hope. The boat was probably hers too. It was probably named for her! She was probably the smuggler-in-chief.

"Time's up," said Michael, herding Susan

indoors as if he were a collie and she some ratty old sheep. "Only a bajillion hours till close. You can do it, Susan."

Mitch had always known what the girl of his dreams would look like. Sometimes, in a magazine, or on television, he'd see the girl that could be her, but in real life, never. In real life, even at college, where some of the girls were pretty staggeringly impressive, he'd never seen the girl of his dreams.

And here she was.

He had always expected her to be blonde, but she was brunette. There was something coppery in her dark hair that surpassed mere blonde; made blondes dull. He had always expected his dream girl to be very fair, and here she was honey tan. *Fair* now seemed pathetic and indoors and fake.

Hope, he thought. I hope she's the one.

He didn't even want to think about what Ginger would say. (The girl is deranged, Mitch. Her computer is not plugged in. Her tapes don't rewind. Her answering machine is off.)

The faint had been more a buckling of the knees. She hadn't really lost consciousness. Just gone down. Mitch, to his everlasting disappointment, had not caught her. She had just suddenly been on the floor. He found himself hoping she'd faint again, so he could be there for her.

He knew what Ginger would say to that, too.

"You *are* Hope," said Mitch, loving that name. He touched her hair again, exactly where he had touched it a few hours ago, and he had the fancy that his prints remained there.

She was sitting up, knees pulled against her chest, trembling.

He was kneeling next to her, as if ready to propose. His father had done that: met Mother, fallen like the proverbial ton of bricks, proposed, and married her in two heartbeats. Part of Mitch wanted to follow in the family romantic footsteps, and part of him was listening to Ginger, who was saying, *Mitch, this girl is nuts.*

What a fool he must seem to Hope's father — this cockamamie story about another boyfriend. He flushed, knowing he'd been an idiot to believe in Hope's memory loss.

He helped Hope up. Tall and athletic she might be, but she still had an aura of vulnerability so intense, he just wanted her to be safely lying down. Preferably with him. At least he knew for sure who she was, and at least he had a date with her. So although the little skit he'd concocted was embarrassing, still, it had worked.

Hope was staring at him with a combination of awe and confusion that Mitch found very attractive. He really was the T-shirt God for Miss Wow Factor.

"Are you feeling better?" he said awkwardly. "I mean, this afternoon — when you didn't know who you were — well, I believed you."

"I still don't know who I am, Mitch," she whispered. "And it's very very weird to find out that I could be one of two people."

Mitch didn't know what to say about that, since the passport made it pretty clear she was Hope Senneth, so he changed the subject. He didn't want to glance at Mr. Senneth because he didn't want to be on the father's team.

"Speaking of this second person," said Mr. Senneth, "although the disappearance of Susan Nevilleson is not my problem at the moment, I need some details about her, Mr. McKenna."

Mitch was not feeling old enough to be called Mr. McKenna. He was feeling stupid and actor-class-y and very sorry he'd said a single thing about the nonexistent boyfriend searching for the not-missing Susan.

"In case the boyfriend does come to talk to

me, what is his name?" Mr. Senneth removed from his inner jacket pocket a slim leather-bound notepad, found a blank page and prepared to take down the details. "Where does he live? Where does this Susan Nevilleson live? What are the phone numbers?"

Mitch couldn't think fast enough to get out of his skit. Feebly he said, "I didn't ask."

"How extraordinary," said Mr. Senneth, closing the little volume very gently, very thoughtfully. "Two disappearing girls in one afternoon? A photograph you instantly recognized? And you skipped essentials like how to get back in touch?"

Mitch felt like a total jerk. "I told him I'd let him know through the police."

Mr. Senneth raised skeptical eyebrows. Mitch felt himself judged, and found lacking. It had to be the father of Hope with whom he was being an idiot, didn't it?

"Then I expect I will next hear from the police," said Mr. Senneth. "And now, Mr. McKenna, if you don't mind, my daughter desperately needs rest. I am sending her to bed."

Actually Mitch didn't mind. Hope did need rest, and he needed to be away from his failed act about the second missing girl. Maybe he would talk it over with Susan. Susan was very clearheaded and understood these things. Or call Ginger. Ginger was sharp as razor blades. She might even help him plan the next act.

Except I don't want to act with Miss Wow Factor, he thought. I want everything real with her. "Good night, Hope," he said, wanting to kiss her.

She was a picture of exhaustion, but she had lost none of her beauty. "Sunday?" he said, and then he couldn't stand waiting till Sunday. "Actually, I'm selling T-shirts all day tomorrow. Saturday's a big day. Stop by? I'll give you a great T."

"Good night, Mitch," said Mr. Senneth.

Hope could practically taste Mitch's nonexistent kiss, the way you could taste bread in the air, when you drove past a bakery.

"Your room," said her father, with only a trace of irony, "is down that hall, Hope."

She obeyed his pointing finger.

There were two rooms off this hall. Both doors were closed. She had to force herself to touch the doorknobs, to trespass, opening other people's bedroom doors.

The first room was surpassingly masculine. Its colors were dark wine and hunter green, like the carpet in the front rooms. Its furniture was heavy and its walls clad in hunting prints.

In the second room, however, a violet carpet lay beneath white furniture painted with green ivy. Wallpaper danced with tiny flowers and creeping vines. Collected mirrors — dozens of tiny glittering ovals, circles, and squares were artistically arranged on one wall. There were twin beds, and if anybody had ever slept in either one, or set something on those bureau tops, or possessed a single CD or cassette to put in that stereo system, it was not evident. It was completely and totally an unused hotel room. Does Kaytha live here? she thought dimly.

Kaytha had had so much personality. Wouldn't she have left a mark of some kind on her room?

Hope was too tired to think anymore about anything. She stood on her side of the closed door, alone, safe, and private.

Breathing room.

And more importantly, bathroom, complete with Jacuzzi. She was tempted, but did not know how to make it work, and used the shower instead, flinging off her clothes and scrubbing away the scariness of the day.

Only soot and sweat came off. The scariness stayed.

Hope meant to stay awake, think about the day, piece together the choices she had made and the choices that had been made for her. She had to concentrate on the existence of that passport. Most of all she had to — or at least ached to — think about Mitch, and love, and T-shirts . . . but the moment her head touched the pillow, she was asleep, and slept like one in a coma.

Like one, thought Kaytha, looking in on her later, who did indeed suffer some traumatic brain damage.

Chapter 6

Mitch actually ran to meet Susan as the restaurant closed. Susan's heart leaped several stories; she could have been atop a skyscraper with joy. "Mitch," she said, beaming at him, forgetting how tired and strained she felt.

"Guess what!" Mitch was larger than life: his arms were thrust outward, his shoulders seemed a yard across, his grin filled the whole block.

"What?" said Susan, wanting those arms to close around her and hug her forever and a day.

Mitch brought his fists up in a victory salute to himself. "I have a date with Miss Amnesia. I'm taking her to the Boston Pops on Sunday." Now he hugged Susan. "She really is Hope Senneth," he confided, as if Susan had been worrying. "Her father showed me her passport. He's a nice enough guy. Kind of a stick, but I was being pretty pushy and he put up with me."

Susan's energy deserted her. She felt short-legged, heavy, and worthless. "She has her memory back, then?"

"No. They're getting a shrink to see her tomorrow."

Tomorrow, thought Susan. Saturday. It'll be even busier in the restaurant on Saturday than it was on Friday. But tomorrow I won't be able to pretend that Mitch's picture is ever going to be in my locket.

For Mitch, the word *romance* was entwined with knights in shining armor; with chivalry and valor and lost causes. He wanted heroic deeds. If Miss Amnesia was indeed an incredibly spoiled brat who faked psychological problems in order to stick it to her rich father, Mitch might not even mind. He might want her in the flames of the dragon's mouth, just so he could rescue her. If she wasn't going to be a memory-loss mystery, she might as well be a deeply disturbed beauty with a dreadful past.

Susan looked at her watch. Two minutes past midnight. It's already tomorrow, she thought.

Mitch babbled on about another girl while he walked Susan to her MTA stop. What was it that made boys so thick? Why couldn't they have an eensy little strand of female DNA so they could see how rude and infuriating it was when they assumed that girls loved being their buddies instead of their dates?

"Bye, Mitch," she said, and he kissed her good night, a brotherly peck that hurt her more than if he had just waved.

The journey to her apartment was not through quaint historic streets on a charming street car, but a dirty, stinking commute. Susan's block was only a few parking spaces from wealth, but nevertheless deep inside squalor. Cities were like that: the shoulders of the rich rubbed against the shoulders of the poor. College students straddled the line.

The house in which Susan had a ground floor apartment was old: brick row house, four-story walkup, grimy little stoop in front, and old, ill-shaped windows. It as not adorable, the way the brick houses around the corner were. It was just there, getting older.

Susan shared the apartment. It certainly wasn't by choice. By choice she would have had a suite at The Jayquith. But Susan's mother worked in a day-care center and Susan's father was on the county road crew. Susan was going to college on a combination of scholarships, loans, and compromises that made her crazy. Having three roommates who were also penniless, hard to get along with, messy, and didn't like the same kind of music — that *really* made Susan crazy. The only good thing about her roomies was they were hardly ever home. Like Susan, what with summer school and jobs and boyfriends (well, they were ahead of Susan on that) and the fact that Boston was very very hot in July and the tiny apartment was not air conditioned — they didn't even have enough fans — well, Susan was the only one home.

I could go out with Ben Franklin on Sunday, she thought, to take my mind off Mitch and Miss Amnesia. But I don't want Ben Franklin. I want studly company. I guess that proves how shallow I really am. If I were deep and complex, I wouldn't adore a man for his biceps.

Susan did not want to spend the night weeping over Mitch. She had done that enough. It was so stupid! Mitch was even more stupid. He'd fallen in love with a girl who didn't know her name, for heaven's sake!

Mitch's college story was that he was an ordinary guy, had to sell T-shirts to stay in school. Susan really did have to sell T-shirts to stay in school (or in her case, wait tables), but there was something about Mitch that didn't ring true. She and Ben Franklin had commented on it from the beginning. Mitch McKenna was somebody else.

They'd even said it to him. Not the way you usually did when somebody was weird — Hey, Mitch, you're something else — but instead — Hey, Mitch, you're some*body* else.

And now Mitch had also fallen for somebody else.

The street was dangerous, especially at this hour. In the summer, people didn't go home to bed early, especially people that girls by themselves ought to worry about. Susan considered herself street smart, and she was careful. Laurie was visiting relatives in Maine this week, while Betsy and Jenny would probably still be out with their boyfriends.

She unlocked the hot, airless apartment just as the phone rang. They had an answering machine, on which her most annoying roomie cooed, "Hel-lo! You have reached the residence of Laurie, Jenny, Betsy, and Suuuuusan! Oh, how we wish we were free to take your call. Please please please please *please* leave your number so we can get right back to you! We adore all our friends! Now wait for our cute little tone!"

Amazingly enough, people did. Susan would have found a different set of friends. It's half past midnight, she thought. What jerk is calling at this hour? To spare herself the shame of listening to the tape yet again, Susan picked up the phone. "Hello?"

Nobody spoke.

Nobody breathed.

Nobody disconnected.

There was a creepy waiting time, during which Susan imagined a thousand horrible things: being stalked, being robbed, being raped, being the victim of a drive-by shooting.

She hung up fast.

How isolated the apartment suddenly seemed. How vulnerable the ground floor windows. How dangerous the sills on which window fans were precariously set.

She watched the phone as if it were a rabid dog, and sure enough, moments later it rang again.

It could be a roomie needing taxi fare, a wrong number, or . . .

She was incapable of listening to a ringing phone. She grabbed it on ring three. "Hello?"

A female voice replied. Articulate, pleasant, friendly. (Probably because she hadn't heard the recording.) "I need to reach Miss Susan Nevilleson, please."

"This is Susan Nevilleson." She was down in the dumps already. Why did she keep on pretending to herself that it was going to be Mitch? The woman probably wanted to sign her up for a different long-distance phone company.

There was a pause, just like the previous call. The caller did not breathe, did not speak. The phone line just hung there.

The fans hummed. The refrigerator clicked. The shades hung at uneven levels, but Susan was illuminated perfectly. She felt as conspicuous as if she were in a glass shower.

The dial tone buzzed in Susan's ear.

Nobody signed you up for a different phone company at this hour. *Was it somebody who found a sick pleasure in learning that Susan was home alone, undefended?*

Susan hated girls who cringed over minor events. She was not going to be like that. It was just a stupid phone call. Not even any words.

Susan tossed her hair, fluffing herself up to her pretend five foot one. To prove she was not scared, she did not pull the shades down and she did not check the locks.

It was the knife that woke Susan up.

An extraordinary, very thin, very glittering knife.

She had the sickening thought that this knife had once hurt another human being. But it was too shiny to have been used.

The knife flickered, and Susan was the human being it was going to hurt.

Susan thought: It's shiny because the owner loves that knife. That knife isn't unused. It's polished.

She obeyed the knife.

She knew from the smile on the face of the knife wielder that everybody obeyed that knife. Always had, always would.

Hope woke up.

She was under extremely heavyweight covers. The sheets were almost slick, a texture she did not associate with sheets, and over them were both a blanket and an ornate bedspread.

Where am I?

Her heart jolted.

She could not remember last night at all. Could not piece together where this strange bed might be. *Where am I?* she thought again.

And then remembered.

Remembering being a completely new kind of thing now. A partial and clouded activity.

It isn't *Where am I?* that matters, she remembered, it's *Who am I?*

Very slowly she eased herself around in the bed. Twin bed. Ivy and violet room, quite dark. A digital clock glowing on a shared bed-table read 8:58 a.m. On the pillow of the other bed rested a tiny blonde head. No face, but a circular shaving of a snake looked back at Hope.

Poised to strike, thought Hope. Not me, please.

The air-conditioning in the hotel was very high, and her nose was actually cold. She burrowed beneath the covers like a child in an attic in February. The sheets, she decided, were silk.

She got up. She had not formulated any plans in her head, but her body seemed to have plans without her: it was hurrying, eager to dress and get going and —

She was entirely naked.

I have no clothes, she thought.

What a good way to keep a prisoner. She was not going to run through the lobbies of The Jayquith naked, no matter what kind of trouble that snake's head proclaimed.

But she was wrong. There, neatly folded, freshly washed, lay yesterday's shorts, shirt, bra, and pants. She put them on, shivering. The air-conditioning was like winter. No wonder heavy blankets had felt so odd — it was still July! She remembered that much. She slid her bare toes into her sandals. It was so cold her feet felt thin.

Several folding shuttered doors lined one wall. She touched one very lightly, and the closet exposed was jammed with clothing: a lot of neutrals and black. Linen, silk, cotton. She touched the closest jacket, white silk, buttonless, with sweatshirt-style sleeves.

It was her size.

Next to the jacket was an indigo blue evening gown. When she took the hanger off the rod, it turned out to be a jumpsuit, wonderfully elegant. A narrow waist with a wide sash and a neckline that swooped, made for fabulous jewelry.

Her size. Her favorite color. It might have been made for her.

Maybe it was made for her.

She hung it back up, shocked.

She felt as if she had stepped through a mirror, and come out into some other silvery world. A world where people actually had suites in The Jayquith, and handsome blond young men fell in love with them in ten seconds, and designer evening dresses magically appeared in closets.

What is real? she thought.

Which of us here is real?

* * *

Ben had arrived on the wharf early because he could think about Susan more at that location. Sometimes he ached for her so much, he actually wanted to stand on her sidewalk, just feasting his eyes on her apartment windows.

Why was Mitch the one with the reputation for romance, when it was Ben with the yearning heart and the aching pit in his gut?

I'm an idiot out of a dated Broadway musical, he thought. *My Fair Lady.* "On the Street Where You Live."

He knew exactly where each of his college classmates stood on the subject of love: Ben loved Susan, Susan loved Mitch, Mitch loved Miss Amnesia. Or more correctly, the idea of Miss Amnesia. You could not really love somebody you did not know.

Susan was such a little person. He could never say out loud that being larger than she was pleased him, because Susan would draw herself up like an animal fluffing its fur to look tougher, and announce coldly that she didn't need a man.

I need a woman, though, thought Ben.

Susan wouldn't be here till eleven-thirty. She worked both lunch and dinner, sometimes an entire twelve or thirteen hours in her desperation to salt away money for the next college year.

Ben hated to see her work so hard. He hated to see the contrast between Susan in the morning, all bounce and laughter, and Susan in the evening, all sag and exhaustion.

He adjusted his little glasses and his fake hair: the sideburns, the wig, the beard. He hooked his fingers in his waistcoat. He saw no tourists and so he wandered over to the restaurant to talk to Michael. Michael was pretty observant too, and knew perfectly well that Ben would want to talk to Susan.

"She called in," said Michael. "She quit."

"*She quit?*" Ben Franklin was stunned. "But —"

Michael shrugged. He was clearly very angry. "She knows how busy we are. Who am I supposed to get to fill in for her? What kind of notice is this? I could not believe it when she called. First thing this morning. She's got another job."

"How could she have another job?" protested Ben. "I just talked to her last night! She would have told me. She couldn't earn more money at any job than she was earning here, what with tips, and the long hours."

Michael shook his head. "Who knows? I think it's Mitch myself."

"You think she's working for Mitch?"

"No, I think she can't stand it that he's fallen so hard for his little memory-loss victim."

The last time Ben remembered feeling so bereft was the day his mother left him at kindergarten. He still remembered the shock of that: *Mommy wasn't staying* and he was with all these human beings he didn't know, abandoned in a room he'd never seen.

Susan quitting made Ben want to quit, too.

Why go through all this, anyway? He didn't even want to talk to Mitch about it, although Mitch was his best friend. Mitch was so thick. He was one of those people who saw straight ahead, and never to the sides; he was a big puppy with big feet and a big sloppy grin. Lovable but dense. He hadn't seen that Susan adored him, or that Ben envied him.

Ben didn't really want to call Susan either. She might spill out her heart, which would consist of telling Ben how wonderful Mitch was. Ben knew that already. Just once in his life, Ben would like to hear how wonderful Ben was. Especially from Susan.

She won't call me, he thought. She won't even think of me.

Michael said, "You want to wait tables, Ben? I'll pay you more than the Park Service."

"No, thanks."

"I don't believe in amnesia," added Michael. "I think the father was telling the truth when he said she was an attention-getting spoiled debutante. I think Mitch is a sucker for beauty."

"Aren't we all?" said Ben quietly. He felt bleak.

Not being able to zip in and out of the restaurant and check Susan out and tell her the day's rumors and nonsense would make the day very very long.

He looked remarkably like the real Ben Franklin.

And just as old.

Kaytha was used to strange assignments but this was stranger than most. She was hot like dry fever just thinking about it. Kaytha loved the soaps; she was just about addicted to two of them. Now she had a soap of her own.

Amnesia.

Pretending sleep, Kaytha studied Hope's face and movements. Pretty as she was, Hope's features were marred by a sort of tic. A nervous twitch of the lip; an occasional shudder. Her gaze was blurry, as if it were her eyes, and not her memory, that were on the blink.

Kaytha could not imagine how this might feel.

Kaytha was very fond of her own memories. She liked going back over them, stroking them as if they were a pet cocker spaniel. Brushing them, cuddling them. It would be a terrible thing to lose your memories. Dr. Patel would love it if Kaytha would stop remembering; that was the purpose of all their sessions: "You have to stop thinking about these things, Kaytha; stop enjoying the memories the way you do. Time to move on, set them aside."

Kaytha had moved on.

But she set nothing aside. Ever.

Mitch opened up his T-shirt wagon. In his entire life he had never felt so cheerful. He was a buoy in the water, clanging and rolling and waiting for Hope. He changed the location of his wagon so that he could see both front and rear exits of The Jayquith.

Mitch was not surprised when Derry came rushing over to him. Derry crewed for *Lady Hope.* Cute and bouncy, she'd been hired as a stewardess.

Wait-on-you crew was always chosen for eagerness. They usually resembled puppies, or Disney World employees. Derry was a perfect fit. Freckled, enthusiastic, and certified in scuba. She was small and therefore took up little space, which was good, because the forward bunks were curved and narrow to fit the shape of the boat. She loved people, gushed over them, never tired of scrubbing windows or mopping decks or garnishing trays of hors d'oeuvres that would never be eaten because the owner and his guests were always on a diet.

Derry's quarters were so small that you would not think she could ever have a possession, and not more than one change of clothing. Yet Derry, like Kaytha, was a T-shirt buyer to the max.

"Hey, Derry," said Mitch, as she ducked under the wagon and came inside with him for a hug.

"I've been fired," she said, and burst into tears.

"What happened?" said Mitch, moving into his consoling role.

There were always several girls in love with Mitch. This had been the situation since school began, since kindergarten. Mitch had never known what he had to offer that other guys didn't. For years, he actually suggested to the girls who didn't interest him other likely and convenient boys, like Jason or Richard.

By junior high, he sensed that you were not supposed to shuffle a girl off on somebody else. If she had a crush on you, she had a crush on you, and there you were.

Mitch was guaranteed a lot of tears. But Mitch was good with tears. The thing was not to run away screaming, which was a reasonable boy's reaction. The thing was to sit there and hand them your handkerchief, which hopefully was unused, and wait till it ended. They did all the talking, and you just had to nod and mop up.

He gave her a crispy white handkerchief, thinking of his bandanna, wanting Hope to keep it forever.

"There was no reason!" cried Derry. "Absolutely none! I've done everything just right! And they need me, Mitch! I was the only woman! They have to have a stewardess aboard because the female guests don't like it when there are only men. The captain promised to give me recommendations. He just said that they couldn't use me anymore." Derry was sobbing and frantic.

Mitch maintained a perfect one-handed hug while he managed a tourist transaction with his other hand. Size XXL Boston skyline in purple.

Derry had curly hair, light brown, streaked

by the sun. It did not compare to Hope's. Nothing compared to Hope's anything. Mitch smoothed Derry's hair back, a nice safe neutral act of comfort, and pretended it was Hope's hair. Hope, with whom he did not want things safe or neutral.

"I didn't even get to go aboard and pack my own things, Mitch!" Derry cried out. "The Senneths just handed my stuff to me! You would have thought I was some executive being fired from some huge company and they thought I would steal their precious formulas. Oh, Mitch, I tried so hard and I thought I was doing so well."

Mitch stared at her. "The Senneths?" He was astonished. "The Senneths own *Lady Hope?*" Wow. Hope not only has a suite at The Jayquith — she's even got a yacht named for her. "Tell me about Hope," he said to Derry.

"She's a wonderful boat. You know how it is when you crew. The owner's hardly ever aboard, and you feel like it's your own boat and you fall in love with her. You use the owner's Jacuzzi and the owner's bed and VCR and the bar and the Wave Runner and —"

"No, no, Hope the person."

"There is no 'Hope the person.' "

"Yes, there is, I met her."

"Well, I haven't met her. I've only met Kaytha the abnormal."

Kaytha Senneth. Mitch frowned, thinking.

She had to be the girl who kept buying T-shirts. The one who flirted with him so annoyingly, and actually seemed to think he would ask her out because she bought a T-shirt every day. She had told him her name at least fifty times. Kaytha. *And given him her phone number.*

Well, well, well. He just might have the phone number of Hope's suite at The Jayquith.

Derry made a face and took a deep breath. "Mitch, I have nowhere to stay." The look of panic in her eyes was as deep as he'd seen yesterday in Hope's. "I'm in Boston, which is a city I don't know at all, we've never sailed here before, we're normally at Deer Isle in the summer and in the Bahamas for winter. I don't know a single person in Boston except you, Mitch."

"Do you have any money?" said Mitch. Money was key.

Derry shook her head no. "I spent everything just yesterday. I went shopping at Quincy Market. They have such cute shops there, Mitch."

Mitch could not stand conversations about

shopping. "I'll ask my friend Susan if you can spend tonight at her place. She has a futon you can roll out. It's totally uncomfortable, but you can start trolling for a new job tomorrow and things will work out, Derry, I'm sure they will."

"Here she comes," muttered Derry, wiping away tears. "I can't stand seeing her. She's creepy. I'm out of here, Mitch."

When Hope was fully dressed, feeling safer, somehow, inside her own clothing, she pulled herself together physically: drawing in her muscles, stiffening her spine, filling her lungs. Now what? she thought.

"Do we go shopping today, Hopester?" said Kaytha in her bright brittle voice. "I adore shopping."

Hope jumped badly. "I thought you were asleep," she said, frightened out of all proportion to the event.

"With you bumbling around pretending you don't know where your own clothing is? Really, Hopesy." Kaytha slid out of her bed. She, too, slept nude, and although she and Hope were the same height, had the same bones, Kaytha was horrifyingly thin.

"Kaytha, aren't you well? You've got to eat

more. I can count your ribs. You look like starvation."

Kaytha said, "I love my body like this."

Hope found herself worried for Kaytha. "You need a big breakfast," said Hope. "How about oatmeal or Wheaties? Certainly orange juice. Eggs and bacon."

"That's disgusting. All that fat? You don't eat like that, do you?"

We live together, thought Hope. She must know how I eat.

"You adore shopping, don't you?" said Kaytha.

"I love shopping," said Hope, which was certainly true, "but I don't have any money."

"You went and lost your purse. Uncle Ken will advance you money till your trust check arrives."

Hope considered that sentence. A very wealthy-sounding sentence. A very tempting sentence. *Uncle Ken will advance you money till your trust check arrives*. Hope drew chilly air into her lungs. Oxygen didn't help.

Kaytha dressed this time in a rather long and puffy flowered skirt with a romantic little crocheted top. Again it did not match the hair style. Her body had a separate personality from her head.

Together the girls walked out of the bedroom and down the hall to the sitting room. Mr. Senneth was reading *The Boston Globe* as he sipped his coffee. "Good morning, girls," he said, not looking up.

This is so strange, thought Hope. I don't even know these people, and they are so used to me, they don't bother to glance my way. Good morning, girls. As if my cousin and I do this all the time, every day.

Of course, this morning, the room *was* slightly familiar. She *had* been here before. She had sat on that couch and looked down at that coffee table. But this morning, her thinking was even more skewed. "I feel as if I should be doing something more important than having coffee," she said to them. "I should be trying to figure out who — I mean what — "

"We know who you are," said Kaytha irritably, "so you can skip that part, Hopester. As for what you are, you are basically very annoying. The thing here is to find your purse."

"My purse," she repeated.

"Hopesy. The necklace? The reason why we're all in Boston?" Kaytha was like a truly put-upon baby-sitter with a truly annoying little kid.

Mr. Senneth said, "Kaytha. Calm down. Hope will think of it in time, I'm sure." He poured coffee for his daughter. It had an odd sweet scent, not like the coffee at home. A flavored fruit scent.

Memory and memory failure came and went like traffic. Her hand shook taking the saucer.

"Sweetheart," said her father gently, "I know it must seem odd to you that I'm not doing anything active. I didn't call Dr. Patel after all, I'm holding off on medication, and we'll wait till your regular schedule for therapy. You see, this is routine with you. If it isn't one scene, it's another."

She stared at her reflection in the highly polished table.

"You really do seem confused, Hope, but you're such a splendid actress, who knows what to think?"

It was not *she* coming toward Mitch, but *they*.

The bronze hair of Hope was easy to spot. Next to her was a head of hair even easier to place. Kaytha. Mitch enjoyed dramatic crazy haircuts, but not on himself or his friends.

Kaytha must be Hope's — what? Sister? They were the same height, and probably the same age, but Kaytha was proof that you could be too rich and too thin. Mitch did not like thin. He did not like the feeling that a girl might expire of starvation on a date.

Mr. Senneth was right behind them. The keeper of the cash, Mitch supposed. These two girls looked as if they could go through a serious amount in one day.

Why hasn't Hope been with Kaytha when she's bought T-shirts from me every day? he thought. Or was she in the background, and that was why I felt I knew her from somewhere? Come on, he thought, Hope could be a lot of things, but never never background.

"Hey!" said Mitch. "It's Miss T-shirt *and* Miss Amnesia!"

Kaytha smiled. "I understand you met my cousin in a typical Hopester way, Mitch."

"Amnesia runs in your family?" said Mitch, laughing.

"Insanity does. We're all having a little trouble believing in the memory loss."

Mitch could not waste time looking at Kaytha when Hope was standing there. She still possessed nothing, was still in yesterday's white shirt and taupe shorts. She still had those long tanned legs he could have spent all day with. It bothered him, though, that she had not changed clothes.

"Mitch!" cried Hope. "Are these your dogs? I've never seen such adorable dogs."

They were small collies: gold, vanilla, and sable. Their muzzles were slim and elegant, and their coats brushed beautifully. They didn't bark. They were well-mannered and although Mitch disliked bringing them to work, he'd had no choice today. It was hard on them: pavement, heat, strangers. It was hard on him, too: getting water, walking them, keeping them in the shade, making sure little touristy urchins didn't roughhouse with them.

"What are their names?" Hope said, laughing with delight. She was on her knees, snuggling with them, kissing them, rubbing her cheek against theirs. The dogs responded affectionately.

Mitch loved a girl who loved his dogs. "Butter and Cotton."

"That's perfect. This one is buttery and melted, and this one is fluffy and cottony."

Mitch's pleasure matched Hope's. There was simply no doubt about it, he decided. Hope and I are meant to be together.

Behind them, Mr. Senneth and Kaytha stood very still.

"Hope and I are going shopping," said Kaytha. "Quincy Market. Hopester claims not to remember Quincy Market."

It was a very old, quite large square in the most historic part of Boston, filled with boutiques and fast food stores and tiny shops and odd little restaurants. Tourists adored it. It was very near: across the busy traffic where the woman had been shot at the other day, and over a few blocks.

"We're going to replace Hopey's purse," added Kaytha. "And we're going to talk steadily about her old purse, jog her memory a little, because it was filled with very important stuff and we have to find it."

Mitch thought that was a strange thing for a city girl to say. If Hope had lost her purse, they were never going to find it. Especially if it contained valuables. And mostly, you didn't lose a purse in the city. You had it stolen from you. And if Hope had lost it, somebody had found it by now, and they weren't going to say so; they were going to keep all those very important things.

"Maybe that's what happened to you, Hope," he said. "Maybe a mugger ripped the purse off your shoulder and shoved you to the ground and you hit your head."

She gave him her blurry look, the one that turned his knees to jelly. "Maybe."

"Move it, Hopes," said her cousin. "We have a mission."

Mitch did not think he had ever seen a girl looking less able to carry out a mission than the confused blurry Hope.

"Have a nice day, Mitch," she said to him.

How could he have a nice day when she was walking away from him?

The two girls crossed the plaza, waited for the WALK lights, heading toward Quincy Market.

"Mitch," said Mr. Senneth, "I'm a little confused about the Susan Nevilleson story."

"Me, too," said Mitch. He had forgotten Mr. Senneth. Hope's father was not going shopping with them after all. He was going to grill Mitch.

"I still need the name of the man asking after her," said Mr. Senneth.

"He never came back," said Mitch, relieved to have a swarm of customers. Pulling the collies back inside the wagon, he looped their leashes over a hook and closed the little swinging door. He sold T-shirts to a whole busload of old ladies. When he dared look in Mr. Senneth's direction, the man was gone.

Good, thought Mitch, letting Mr. Senneth go from his thoughts as well as his sight. I can't believe I'm letting Hope wander off without me. I have to get my priorities in order.

He bellowed at the top of his lungs. "Derry! Derry!"

"I'm right here," she said. "I was crouching behind the wagon."

"You're weird."

"I'm sane. Kaytha's weird."

"Derry, sell T-shirts for me? I want to go shopping with the girls."

"Aren't you afraid I'll skip town with your inventory?"

"I wish you would. I'm pretty sick of Boston cotton." Mitch showed her the details and ran. The girls could vanish into the rabbit warrens of Boston very easily. He wanted to catch up with them, spend the day with them, protect Hope from the world.

"Mitch!" shrieked Derry.

"What?"

"You didn't tell me this job included dog sitting. Take these beasts with you!"

Mitch came back in a huff. He didn't care whether Derry had a place to sleep now or not. Beasts, indeed. Butter and Cotton were the finest dogs in Boston. Perhaps the world.

Although two collies were certainly going to clutter up a day with Hope, he gave his dogs orders, and they panted agreeably.

The girls hadn't gotten far. They were right

by Faneuil Hall, half listening to a parks guard discuss the Revolution.

"I know you, Hopey," Kaytha was saying. "You cannot have lost it. You just want it for yourself. Where is the necklace, Hopester? You *couldn't* really have lost it," she repeated, as if she meant this: Losing the necklace was physically impossible. As if it was completely unthinkable for Hope to have lost this necklace.

Necklace, thought Mitch. Must have been some necklace. They're more worried about that than they are about Hope losing her memory.

For some reason, "necklace" sounded familiar to him. As if he had been thinking about necklaces lately. But that was impossible. Mitch never thought about jewelry. Only about the women who wore it. "Hi, girls!"

When they turned and smiled, Mitch knew he was in familiar trouble. Both Kaytha and Hope were very glad to see him. Story of his life. Too many girls in love at the same time. Cousins under the same hotel roof — not to mention yacht — would be much harder to separate.

Mitch concentrated on giving two girls a wonderful Saturday, while convincing one to vanish.

Chapter 7

The sun backlit Mitch's blond hair. He glowed like a young god of health and beauty.

I can't believe, thought Hope, that on top of everything else, I am falling in love.

The interior of her mind was now so confusing, she decided not even to use it. She would just walk along, enjoy herself, smile into the sun, admire the lovely dogs, and let her heart go to their handsome owner.

Mitch transferred Butter's leash to Hope, and Cotton's leash to Kaytha. They walked girl and dog, man, girl and dog, filling the sidewalk.

"Somebody should paint us," said Hope, turning to laugh at the pretty picture the five of them made. "I bet we're the most attractive group in Boston." She had to kneel and hug her collie for a moment. Butter kissed her hand. "Don't you love that in dogs?" she said to Mitch. "How they want to become friends so quickly? How they're willing to trust in you, that you're terrific, and worthy of them?"

In the shafts of sunlight, like the smiles of fate, they gazed upon each other. Hope discarded her mental list of what she ought to be thinking about, and thought only of Mitch. It was Kaytha who was closest to Mitch, and had wrapped her free arm around Mitch's, but she might have been a passing toddler, for all that he noticed her.

Quincy Market was teeming with people. Crowds jammed the little outdoor booths. Sidewalk restaurants sold coffee, croissants, and blueberry everything. Baby strollers bumped over cobbled streets. Junior high kids traveled in packs. High school boys stole looks at Hope.

"The whole city is developing a crush on you," murmured Mitch.

Kaytha paused in front of a women's boutique whose clothing was so absurd, and yet so stunning, that Hope could not imagine ever wearing it anywhere, and was dying to try it on and invent someplace to wear it. Kaytha seemed the least likely woman in all Boston this Saturday to put that on her body.

The collies pressed on, toward shade and sitting down.

"Aren't those darling?" cried Kaytha, halting next at a tiny outdoor shop.

Hope could not imagine a person who cut her hair the way Kaytha did, finding anything darling, or wanting to. "Those are for ponytails," said Hope.

"Just because I don't have any hair doesn't mean I can't admire scrunchies and hair clips. Look at that cute little teabag."

"Why," said Mitch, "would any girl want to wear a teabag in her hair?"

"Boston Tea Party?" reminded Kaytha. "You who sell four different Tea Party T-shirts ought to know the meaning of tea in this town." Kaytha bought herself a tea bag pin.

In the next booth, jewelry made from old-fashioned bottle caps lay in rows on black velvet. The names of long-vanished soda brands were printed in bright fifties colors. Somebody had turned the caps into necklaces, earrings, bracelets, and key rings. Hope touched them wonderingly. This was a fad somewhere, but not where she had ever seen it. Where have I seen things? she thought. What should I be seeing right now?

"Looking at the necklaces?" said Kaytha. Her eyes were strange and bright. "Is that the kind of necklace you like?" It seemed to Hope that she was emphasizing the word *necklace* very strongly. As if it were a password. As if this whole walk, everything Kaytha and Mitch and Butter and Cotton did with her was a conceit, a trick: All that mattered was their missing necklace.

Hope tightened both hands on Butter's leash, like a little kid caught touching in a museum.

"Would you like one?" said Kaytha.

"No, no," she said, embarrassed. "I don't have any money."

"You have pots of money. I'll buy it for you," said Kaytha. "You can pay me back."

"No, no. No, thank you."

"Where *is* your purse, Hopey?"

"I don't know, Kaytha. I don't even know if I'm Hopey."

"Who else would you be?" said Kaytha. "Give me a name."

It was not yet noon, but the city was very hot. And Kaytha, too, seemed overheated. She was burning with fevers. Love and greed and fear.

"Let's set this up differently," said Mitch. "Let's you tell us all about Hope, Kaytha, and see if it flicks a switch as she listens."

"Hopester's switches are usually on dim,"

said Kaytha. She handed Cotton's leash over to Hope, so Hope held both dogs, and Kaytha instead held both of Mitch's hands.

Her crimson fingernails looked too long and too hard to be real. Was there such a thing as fake fingernails? Mitch tried, and failed, to imagine gluing red nails onto his big broad hands.

"I am not dim!" said Hope, insulted. Kaytha gave her a funny cousinly look and Hope found herself smiling back. "Kaytha, please tell me about myself."

Kaytha shook her head. "That means I go along with the whole amnesia thing, and I don't, Hopey, you know that. You're making it up. I think I know why, too."

"Why?" said Mitch immediately. "Explain it to me, too, Kaytha. Why would she make it up?"

"Because she snitched a very valuable necklace of Uncle Ken's and now she's lost it. In typical dumb pointless Hopester fashion, she's decided to pretend she isn't even Hope, or can't remember being Hope." Kaytha rolled her eyes. She was wearing a tremendous amount of makeup. Great blue shadows arched over her little green eyes.

"I don't steal," said Hope quickly.

"How do you know?" demanded Kaytha. "If you claim not to remember being Hope Senneth, then how do you know for sure what disgusting things Hope Senneth does — or doesn't do?"

Hope had no argument for that. She flushed.

Streets narrowed and buildings closed in. They entered a lovely brick-walled garden, with an unused fountain and many plaques. Hope wanted to pause, and read all the inscriptions, stop and think about the men who created the Revolution, which would certainly be easier than thinking about whether she was a thief. But the three of them strolled on, as if they often went out together.

"Are you all right, Hope?" said Mitch suddenly.

Or was it sudden? She felt as if she had drifted, been drifting a long time, and people had been staring at her without her even knowing. Hope's smile faded like color in the sun, and a note of fear penetrated her voice. "It isn't coming back, Mitch. None of it." She tried to find the smile again. "The clothes fit me. People recognize me. But . . ."

She landed him with that close-to-tears look. He touched her hair a third time. It might look like bronze, but it felt like silk. He wondered if they would always be together, and he would always keep count of the number of times he had touched her hair.

"Hopester is fine," said Kaytha angrily. "Just obnoxious as always. Starting scenes and not finishing them."

Kaytha was not in love with her cousin. In fact, if Mitch had to define it, he'd say Kaytha was in hate. Under the oppressive sun, Mitch shivered slightly.

"I suppose," said Kaytha, her voice high and thin, sort of floating above the action, "that Hope thinks Uncle Ken won't kill her if she can't remember who she is."

"And will Uncle Ken kill her?" Mitch wanted to know.

"Definitely. She has only a few days to live at best."

Mitch had the sick sensation that Kaytha meant this.

"Which is why, Hopesy," said Kaytha sharply, "I think you should 'fess up. Tell me where you put the necklace. I'll get it back to Uncle Ken and you won't get punished. Or at least, not too much."

They walked past burial grounds and churches. They walked under lovely old trees and past a hundred ice cream vendors. They passed the beautiful old State House and stared across the green expanse that was Boston Common.

Hope took refuge in silence. What if Mitch wandered off, never to be seen again, now that he had a picture of her as a thief? Am I a thief? she thought. Does that define me? A common, garden-variety thief? But what can I do about it? How can I get that necklace back?

"Want to ride on the swan boat, Hope?" said Mitch.

"What is a swan boat?" How romantic it sounded! Would they sit together among feathers, pillowed in white down? Would tiny blue waves tickle their ankles?

Kaytha said, "Just inviting Miss Amnesia, are you?"

"Of course not. I want to take both of you on the swan boat."

The dogs could see grass and were excited. They needed to run. "Come on!" said Hope. "Let's race! I'll win!" She took off, dogs flying beside her, holding their leashes out on either side to prevent tangling herself or them. Mitch caught up quickly and easily, and the two floated over the wide public lawns, swooping and curving, playing at tag and dance.

Kaytha screamed for them to wait up, like a five-year-old left behind.

"She has a lot of nicknames for you," said Mitch. "Don't you have any for her?"

"Mitch, I don't remember her, never mind her nicknames."

They stared at each other. The dogs whimpered, wanting to run more.

"I can't make up my mind about you," said Hope.

He laughed. "You're not the one who gets to say that."

"I mean it. You're so many characters. Are you acting, or did you really fall for me so fast?"

Oh! thought Mitch, *girls!* It isn't the acting she cares about — it's whether I mean it. "I really fell for you that fast," he promised her. "And I'm still falling. You're incredibly beautiful. And it's pretty darn unusual; rich and a world traveler and living at The Jayquith — and not remembering yourself to top it off. What does that feel like inside?"

"I'd rather talk about you," she said quickly. "Tell me what it's like to be a guy who can call Mother and get the keys to The Jayquith."

He did not attempt to answer that. He said, "Hope?"

"Mmm?"

"Are you for real?"

"You don't believe me?"

"No, actually, I don't. Kaytha is weird, letting you go out shopping for the day if you're hurt. But the other story, that you're a nutcase spoiled brat — it doesn't fit you! And the necklace story is weirdest of all."

"I am a nutcase spoiled brat."

Her answers were too quick, too flippant. "I don't believe that," said Mitch. Or is it that I can't bear believing that? I don't want her to be off center, off base, I want her to be just right, all the way through.

"Tell me the truth, Hope." Slowly, he moved closer and closer to Hope, and then he was bending, so that their faces were only a fraction of an inch apart, and his lips could all but feel hers.

"Rats," said Mitch, straightening up, "here comes Kaytha."

Hope giggled. It was such a cute, fifties kind of expletive: *rats!* "Next, you'll be saying, 'Aw shucks,' " she whispered.

"No. Next I'll be saying, Kiss me."

Hope stared at him: the precious beauty of him, mixed with such wholesomeness, as if Mitch had come into the world, and would go out of the world, a good thoroughly decent person. Just don't let him go out of my world! she prayed. "I didn't mean to fall in love," she whispered, for that was the only truth she could give right now.

"I don't think anybody does," said Mitch, although this was a complete lie, because he had always planned to fall in love.

Kaytha caught up. She was terribly out of breath, even though she had not run, only walked quickly.

How thin and weak she is, thought Mitch, comparing her very unfavorably with the athletic Hope. I could whip Kaytha with restaurant toothpicks, or even the mints.

They crossed Charles Street to the Public Garden. The swan boats were quite large. They didn't seem to have motors, but moved soundlessly over the water. Passengers sat on a flat gondola, while the swan herself rode in back, like a great white queen.

Hope's heart jumped.

Where the crowds lined up to buy tickets, along the edges of the lovely placid little lake, was something she needed.

Hope held her breath. She said, "Mitch, you and Kaytha go. It looks so romantic. I'll wait on a bench."

It was clean. That was the only thing she was sure of. And had a distinctive smell. But she could not identify it.

It had motion. A strange swaying that was completely unfamiliar.

She herself could not see. Could not talk. Could not move. She could only hear.

Fear rippled through Susan, her teeth chattered behind her sealed lips. Where am I? What is going on?

How were you supposed to function when you couldn't move or talk? How were you supposed to know what was going on when you couldn't see? So this was how Miss Amnesia had felt, trapped in the meaninglessness of her own mind, with nothing to go by.

Susan held onto herself. She was a problem solver. She would solve this one. It was merely a matter of thinking calmly.

What reasons could there be? Was she in a hospital? Had she been in a terrible accident; was she in traction, in casts? Was her jaw wired together, and had she had eye surgery as well?

If she'd been hurt that much, she'd be in pain. Serious pain.

All I'm doing is lying here, she thought. And the smell — it's — varnish, I think. Old-fashioned varnish. Where do people use varnish? Refinishing furniture?

She tried to arch her back, and succeeded. She tried to move her hands and didn't. Okay, her fingers were free; it was her wrists that didn't move, and the feeling was not metal, not cord, not rope.

I'm tied up, thought Susan. I'm tied up with some unbreakable-even-with-sledge-hammers-from-outer-space plastic.

And I'm gagged. With tape. I can feel it pulling at my skin. I've been taped shut.

She wiggled her eyebrows and cheeks and turned her head back and forth and back and forth. She was blindfolded, not with the tape on her mouth, but with fabric. You can't screw a blindfold down. If she kept this up, rubbing her head, arching her eyebrows, she was eventually going to get the blindfold off.

And see what?

Who would do this to me? What does he have in mind? What have they already done — when I wasn't awake to know it?

Where am I?

And can I ever get home?

Kaytha was blinded by Mitch McKenna. He was so incredibly handsome.

It had been worth all those little purchases from him, the flirting, the endless giving of her phone number, slowly awakening him from that thick slumber in which boys so often lay.

Boys were wonderful, and life without them was bland, but they were so dense.

Kaytha saw herself dancing with Mitch, sailing with Mitch, making love to Mitch.

She wanted his big firm hand resting on the bristles of her short hair, letting it tickle his palm.

They sat on a bench for two, Kaytha much closer to Mitch than necessary. He was in his usual jeans and T and everything about him was absolutely, totally right.

For a minute she worried about leaving Hope. Her job, her assignment, was not to leave Hope for a moment. But how could she be expected to baby-sit Hope when she had a chance at Mitch?

Mitch chattered about boats he had known. Big boats, little boats, power boats, sailboats.

Kaytha picked up his hand and examined each of his fingers separately, tracing the lines on his palm.

Mitch took his hand back, and folded his arms across his chest. "I always wanted to have this for a summer job, you know, Kaytha."

"What?"

"Pedaling a swan boat."

"You're kidding," said Kaytha. He really was

kind of dumb. Selling T-shirts or pedaling swan boats were his life goals? On the other hand, he could crew on *Lady Hope,* and that way Kaytha would have him handy.

"I like using my muscles," said Mitch, "and that's how the boat is powered. The legs of a college boy." Mitch babbled. He was amazed at how badly hurt the heart of this college boy was right now. How could Hope, right after she said, *I didn't mean to fall in love,* next tell him that since the swan boat was romantic, he should take Kaytha? What normal American boy would want to be near Kaytha? Especially with Hope for contrast? Had she forgotten what she looked like, along with everything else?

Or had Hope not really fallen in love with Mitch?

What if Hope was more similar to him than he wanted? What if boys fell for her in such droves that she was accustomed to signing them off to other girls? Maybe her affection for Kaytha was enough that she'd just deal Mitch to her cousin like a deck of cards. Who was Hope — the spoiled brat, the amnesiac, the thief?

I don't even care, he thought, I just want to be with her.

My life is working out just like my father's.

Love at first sight, and then — well, no. I don't want a wedding next week. But I sure want to go on a date!

It seemed reasonable to Mitch McKenna to trust Hope's cousin with a fact. He took both Kaytha's hands in his and completely misinterpreted her softened look. "I'm really crazy about her, Kaytha. Please talk to me about Hope. I'm dying to know everything there is to know about her."

Kaytha withdrew her hands. She stared at him. "Are you *dying to?*" she asked in a raw voice. A strange expression crossed her face . . . as if she might just allow Mitch to have that very wish.

"No, I asked Betsy, too," said Laurie. "None of us has seen Susan lately, Rusty." Laurie didn't sound interested in seeing Susan later, either.

"But she must be somewhere," objected Ben Franklin.

"I'm sure she is, Rusty," said Laurie, in the voice of one who can just barely waste her valuable time with the slug telephoning her. "But she's a grown woman and she'll come home when she comes home. As for Mitch's little friend Derry, forget it. I'm not interested in having her sleep over here. I mean, it's hard enough to get along with Betsy and Jenny."

"Is it hard to get along with Susan?" asked Ben Franklin.

"It's impossible to get along with Susan," said Laurie.

"Will you tell her to call me when she gets in?"

"I'm never here, Rusty. I'll leave her a note. She might see it."

Ben Franklin never wished ill on people, but he could not help hoping that if there were to be a mugging that night, Laurie would be the victim.

It did not bother him at all that Susan was impossible to get along with. In fact, it made her seem more of a sterling character to Ben Franklin: unyielding and tough.

The blindfold lay halfway across her face, annoying one eye terribly but leaving the other free to open and close.

She was in a tiny bunk, incredibly narrow, with a bend in it, as if made for something other than humans. There were no windows. The bunk was curtained, for privacy, perhaps, and on the other side of it, Susan could hear somebody crying. It was muffled. Either the weeping person was far away, or stifling his sobs in a pillow.

The tape was driving her crazy. It yanked at the tiny, hitherto unnoticeable hairs along her lip and cheek. It was drying out her lips like the worst winter wind on a ski slope. She started wetting the tape with spit, hoping to soften the glue, free up some of her mouth.

I won't cry, thought Susan. I won't cry.

She cried.

Under the tape it sounded perfectly normal. You could cry without having your mouth open.

"Are you awake?" said a woman on the other side of the curtain.

Susan froze.

She did not necessarily want notice, did she? Because what would they do to her once she was awake?

Poor Miss Amnesia, thought Susan. I'm sorry I was suspicious. I'm sorry I was skeptical. How terrified she must have been, without any landmarks! Going home with people she didn't know, to a room she didn't remember!

But I'd rather be in her position. At least she could see. And run if she had to.

Susan looked at her wrists. A pale fleshy circle of plastic, like a heavy bracelet, circled each wrist: two separate pairs of handcuffs, each fastened to a sort of brass railing on the edge of the bunk.

I couldn't run if I wanted to, thought Susan Nevilleson. Whatever they do to me, I have to lie here and let happen.

A phone booth.

The swan boat moved so slowly over the glassy blue pond. Kaytha and Mitch waved. Hope waved back. Go, go, go, she thought at them.

She watched the phone booth. It was not a booth, actually, just three little phone boxes facing out on a pole. For some tourists, they ruined the ambiance of the Garden with their gleaming metal surfaces. Hope thought they were beautiful.

The swan boat turned very slowly and, very slowly, a large leaf-laden maple tree came between her and the two riders who mattered.

Hope gathered the leashes of Butter and Cotton and headed for the phone booth.

"You've already acquired his dogs?" said Mr. Senneth, smiling. "Hope, you move very quickly."

She whirled, horrified by his presence. Had he followed them? He must have!

"Don't be afraid," he said. "Really, Hope,

you are overreacting to everything these days."

"Did you follow me?"

"Of course. Hope, you're a very sick girl. I'm trying to be a very understanding father, but it isn't easy."

He took Cotton's leash and they walked out on the grass and circled two huge blooming shrubs. The dogs were ecstatic. The scents must have been many and unusual.

Was she very fortunate that Mr. Senneth had not realized she was heading for a telephone? Or very unfortunate?

Hope only wished she could read what to do next as easily as the dogs could read those bushes.

Her own personal T-shirt god — *in love with somebody else.*

Kaytha had been jealous before in her life. It was a major reason why she disliked school. She was richer than most of them, with a life infinitely more interesting and more complex, but other girls were sometimes prettier and almost always had more friends.

The swan boat returned to the shore. Mitch loped off, leaving Kaytha behind for a second time. Mitch did not turn to see how she was doing, and did not ask if she'd had a good time. He went straight to Hope, and the two dogs pranced and barked, in the way of dogs frantically, terrifically, hugely glad to see their master. Mitch hardly noticed his collies, but was enthralled by Hope. He seemed a little bit afraid of her, as if touching her hair would entangle him in more than a romance.

Kaytha's jealousy was rising and expanding.

How she loved that feeling.

She had never tried drugs, but they must be just like this: a taking over. Where you became the container, and not the person.

Kaytha preferred being a container. When you were being a person, there were so many difficulties.

She let herself go toward the jealousy. It was hot and wonderful and cruel and fulfilling.

Kaytha never regretted anything. She could not recall feeling sorry for any action at any time. What happened, happened. Kaytha would deal.

And Kaytha always dealt herself a winning hand.

Mr. Senneth transferred Cotton's leash back to Mitch, and then took Butter's leash from Hope and handed that also to Mitch. "The girls and I have things to do," he said courteously.

He pointed to a gray limousine waiting by the curb, over on Charles Street.

Mitch held the leashes loosely, and the dogs sat on the green, green grass. The trio deserved to be painted, or at least photographed. They were achingly beautiful.

"I'll see you Sunday night," he said to Hope. He didn't want her to go.

"Yes." She wanted to say more; much much more; but Kaytha and Mr. Senneth were pushing, maneuvering her away from him. "Sunday night," she promised.

"The Boston Pops," he said.

"*Indiana Jones,*" she said. "*Superman.*"

The distance between them widened.

"*Jurassic Park!*" he yelled.

"*E.T.!*" she shouted.

Mr. Senneth said, "Hope. Please."

"You skipped *Raiders of the Lost Ark,*" said Kaytha.

But they were too far apart for Hope to yell anymore. She waved at Mitch. He hadn't moved. Nor had the dogs. A tourist took the photograph that Hope wanted. *What if I never see him again?* she thought. *What if* — but of course I will. We have a date.

They reached the limousine.

It was a gray prison, an underwater chamber. "Where are we going?" she said, suddenly choked with fear. *I can't go with them. I've got to run back to Mitch, I have to —*

"Don't be afraid," said Mr. Senneth mildly.

Kaytha stretched and flexed her long fingers, with their far too large crimson fingernails. She smiled down at her tucked-in fist. She spread her fingers, as if they were a selection of weapons, and then she smiled at Hope.

And Hope was afraid.

Chapter 8

Susan's mouth ached. She felt like a beauty queen who had been smiling for days. But she had finally gotten most of the tape off her mouth. What a relief to be able to suck in lots of air at one time! Not have that horrible sense that if she coughed or panicked, she might suffocate.

It turned out there was such a thing as momentary amnesia, either from shock or physical trauma. Like Hope, she had been too stunned by events to pull her mind into gear.

Susan could not remember being brought here. She assumed they had chloroformed her, a possibility she knew only from old movies. Carrying her on board, they probably explained to people that she was a drunk guest. Probably everybody had laughed, knowing what drunken guests were like.

Susan was not laughing.

She did physical things, centering herself: it was like yoga, except she was removing blindfolds and tape instead of reaching meditative positions.

They were talking now, she and the woman she could not see.

They were both prisoners. And the rolling sensation she had never experienced was water; they were on board a boat.

Susan could find nothing in it: no facts, no understanding, no clues, and, most horribly of all, no hope.

"But what," said Susan, "is going on?"

"We're going to die," said the woman on the bunk opposite.

Soft warm leather, like doeskin, the color of alpine reindeer, lined the limousine. She stroked it, and then held herself still, wondering if the chauffeur would really take them to the hotel.

Mr. Senneth became involved with his Powerbook, fingers barely lifting as they typed. Kaytha fondled an old-fashioned ivory hair comb she had taken from her purse.

The dark glass windows of the limousine removed them from the rest of the world as sunglasses separate one's eyes from the crowd's. The interior seemed timeless, placeless. And she herself, nameless. Faceless.

She was a person literally along for the ride, and then, unexpectedly, the ride ended. She realized that she had not thought she would ever see The Jayquith again.

Doormen sprang forward, opening doors with a flourish. It would be fun, momentarily, at least, to strut in such gaudy uniforms. The Senneths, however, did not enter The Jayquith.

Mr. Senneth took Hope's elbow, elegantly, as if escorting her to her chair at a banquet. "Don't be nervous," he said. "We're just going to the boat instead."

"The boat?" she repeated.

"We'll be more private on the boat."

"Boat" conjured up some little dinghy; some unstable wooden thing banging up against an old sagging deck.

They walked across the plaza, past the wagon where someone else sold T-shirts, past the history guides and the hotdog vendors. Past the commuter boat, past the wedding-for-hire boat, past a trim little sailboat tied up so the owners could have dinner at one of the wharf restaurants, and up to a magnificent private motor yacht.

The *Lady Hope*. A truly serious yacht. So feminine. No wonder they called boats "she." So graceful you wanted to take her dancing. Long curving lines and sleekly rising cabins. Her windows, like the limousine's, were of dark glass so no one could see in. Her paint was deep, rich, flag blue. A clear coat, like nail polish, made her glitter in the sun. She might have been a precious stone from a far country. In lacy script, her name said: *Lady Hope*. Her tender, lying on a sundeck, was *More Hope*.

No fewer than four signs guarded her:

PRIVATE.

NO TRESPASSING.

NOT A TOUR BOAT.

DO NOT ATTEMPT TO BOARD.

But they were boarding.

A pink-cheeked young man, so sunburned he glowed, appeared on the deck. "Good evening, Mr. Senneth," he said, smiling. "Good evening, Miss Senneth," he said jointly to Kaytha and Hope. He wore a uniform, summer white, crisp with little gold epaulets. "Lady Hope" was embroidered on his pocket and his name, "Billy," embroidered just below.

Portable metal chairs were hooked over the edge of the boat. The sunburnt boy steadied the steps.

"This boat," she said. "Is she — named for me?"

How strange to look into the eyes of this man, her father, to find out if he bought and sailed and named yachts *for her!*

"Of course she's named for you," said Kender Senneth. "You are my life." He laughed ruefully. "And not an easy life, I assure you."

The wooden dock creaked loudly, as if breaking up. The yacht bumped against plastic globes that protected her sides from scraping. Waves lifted the stairs right off the dock. The boat moved several inches away, and then gently back.

Kaytha kicked her shoes off and into a wicker basket lying at the foot of the steps. Kender Senneth slipped out of his in the same way.

How extraordinary. Hope stared at the shoes. She could think of no ritual in America that required the removal of shoes. She deposited her sandals into the growing pile of footwear in the basket. Her bare feet followed his socks up the nearly vertical stairs and onto the deck of *Lady Hope.* She couldn't find handholds.

I'll fall, thought Hope. I'll fall between the dock and the boat. Be crushed and left for crabs to chew on.

Kaytha was laughing at her.

She was swamped in a sense of no control. Events had swirled around her, like the tornado around Dorothy in Kansas. Momentum was rushing her from one impossible setting to another.

I want to leave! thought Hope.

As if it were a stage, and she didn't want the part after all, she looked back over her shoulder, searching for the wings and the exits.

But the sunburnt boy steadied her, the father grabbed her hand, and she was brought aboard.

Wooden decks glistened as if it had just rained. Not a scuff nor a scratch marred the entire ninety-foot length. Think of growing up on a yacht like this! There was such beauty in the Senneths' lives. Such perfection.

She imagined eight-year-olds, skidding in a game of stocking-footed tag around and around the deck. She imagined playing treasure island, and pirates, and walk-the-plank off this boat.

Am I imagining, she thought . . .

. . . *or have I done it?*

It took Mitch considerably longer to cross town. The collies were exhausted and hot, and their feet hurt. The pavement was hot and broken, and hurt their feet even more. They wagged their tails sadly at him, and tried to be nice about it.

Mitch gave up and took a taxi.

Butter and Cotton loved the backseat of cars, and joyfully stuck their noses out the cracked windows, savoring the world through its windblown scents. He hugged them both, and they wagged their entire bodies in the sheer and absolute delight of being loved.

Back at the T-shirt wagon, Derry was doing an extremely poor job selling. "I hate people," Derry confided.

"How can you be a stewardess on a yacht and hate people?"

"Oh, those people. They're nice, clean, rich, well-spoken people. Your T-shirts seem to appeal exclusively to mean, dirty, poor, foul-mouthed people."

Mitch was insulted. "Just for that, you have to sell another hour. I want to run over and talk to Ben Franklin."

"Another hour?" cried Derry.

"Hell lasts longer," Mitch assured her.

Derry muttered to herself and was immediately surrounded by kindred spirits, except that they were muttering for T-shirts.

Ben Franklin and Michael the headwaiter were outside the restaurant while Michael had a cigarette and Ben Franklin told him how bad it was for his health.

"Mitch!" said Ben gladly. "Have you seen Susan? Did she call you?" For once Ben wouldn't mind — well, not too much — if Susan had called Mitch. He was excessively worried about her, and he knew it, but she was such a solid person. So reliable. It wasn't like her to abandon a job.

"No," said Mitch, with the blank air of one who never thought about Susan. Like her roomies. Ben felt a surge of anger at Mitch. Why couldn't he appreciate what kind of girl had fallen for him?

"She quit the restaurant," said Michael, "and Ben's worried about her. But she called in, Ben. I mean, she isn't dead in an alley somewhere. I heard from her."

Ben waited for Mitch to express concern but he didn't. "People quit their jobs all the time," said Mitch. "She'll drop by in a day or two and let us know what she's up to. And if she doesn't, we're in the same drama class in September."

September! Mitch actually expected Ben to wonder until September where Susan was?

"Your Miss Amnesia boarded *Lady Hope,* by the way," Michael said to Mitch. He pointed through the tourists, ticket stands, and masts to the brilliant blue hull. "And it was weird. I don't think Hope has ever boarded a boat before. She didn't know how."

Mitch blinked. A boat named for her? A boat her cousin ran on and off so easily? "But it's hers," he said. "Of course she knows how to board the boat."

"There's something fishy about that boat," said Michael.

Ben laughed. " 'Fishy,' meaning people who go out to sea to catch a tuna? That is the least fishy boat I can think of. That kind of yacht is for parties. For fund-raisings. Gala events where the women got their gowns in France."

"That's true," agreed Michael. "In fact, they're having a huge event tonight. Everybody's been notified. Special parking. People are going to be allowed to drive right up on the plaza and leave their Rolls-Royces and Mercedes and Jaguars here."

So those are the plans, thought Mitch. So that's why Mr. Senneth collected Kaytha and Hope — they have to get ready for this gala event that I'm not invited to.

He was extremely hurt, even though there was absolutely no reason to have invited a T-shirt acquaintance, and many reasons not to.

He told himself not to think about crashing the party.

"Susan and I were talking about *Lady Hope* last night," said Michael. "We agreed the Senneths are drug dealers."

Mitch was shocked. Drugs? His beautiful Hope? Her distinguished father? The weird cousin, yes, she definitely had that I'll-try-any-pharmaceutical-on-earth look to her. "Hope is a pawn in a drug deal?" he said, frowning at Michael's idea. "But then, what's with the memory loss?"

"Whoa," said Michael. "I don't think Miss Amnesia is a pawn in anything. What I can imagine is Mr. Senneth exchanging money with some very well-to-do addicts who aren't going down an inner-city alley to buy." Michael shrugged. "But maybe they're clean. After all, *Lady Hope* is clearly a toy boat."

"*Toy?*" said Mitch, outraged. "How dare you — "

"Every toy in the world is tied down on that upper deck, Mitch, just waiting for some athletic little guest to use. They've got two Wave Runners, scuba equipment, Jet Skis, snorkeling gear, a Sunfish, every kind of fishing gear in the hemisphere, old-fashioned water skis, and a Boston Whaler to pull you. I bet they've got fax, computer, modems, radar, depth sounder, loran, a chef instead of a mere cook, closed-circuit security monitors. It's the kind of boat multimillionaires charter for a season."

"Wow," said Ben. "I say definitely board her. See if we can play with their toys. At least get a party invitation."

"You can't board *Lady Hope.* They have a guard," said Michael.

"They have a deckhand," said Mitch, "whose cutesy little shirt has cutesy little pretend military insignia. It's some college kid just like us."

He grinned at his best friend. "I'm crashing it. What are they going to do about it? Throw me in the harbor? Call the police?"

"Cancel your date with Miss Amnesia is more like it," said Ben Franklin.

Hope would have expected a ship's living quarters to be cramped, with low ceilings and salt-crusted portholes. But the salon was spacious and airy, with large high windows overlooking the wharf.

The *Lady Hope*'s salon was ringed with sofas, built-in half-moons of luxury. The carpet underfoot was thick as a goosedown jacket . . . and pure white. No wonder shoes were forbidden. Both white carpet and varnished deck would be destroyed by gritty-bottomed city shoes.

The air-conditioning was like a gift. You

could sit within the perfection of *Lady Hope,* floating on the water, and experience no weather whatsoever: no heat, no humidity, no sun. But there it lay in front of you, sparkling and without flaw, for money — the wealth that built *Lady Hope* — kept passengers safe from flaws.

The pink-cheeked Billy served drinks in stemmed crystal glasses. Hers, with a twist of lime, was clear and bubbly. Designer water.

Her thoughts were as shaken as Kender Senneth's drink.

Kender Senneth belonged on such a ship, being served by a steward in a monogrammed shirt, sending faxes from the wheelroom, and she was sure that any minute he would exchange his suit for something casual, something wonderful, and probably also white, probably so fashionable she would hardly recognize it.

Who could be afraid in such a place, where the only thing that could happen to you was too much pampering?

Food appeared, as exotic as edible sculpture. It didn't look like something people ate, but like an artistic window display.

The salon was covered by an immense map of the waters themselves: rocks and shoals, currents and channels. Hope studied it without learning anything.

It was strange to know so much, and at the same time so little.

The steward shifted his weight. A servant. She did not think she had ever come across a real-life servant. Barely out of his teens, in his perky uniform he might have been a kid ready for Halloween night. She had a creepy flash of memory: she had seen him before — dressed differently — dressed . . . ?

The chef, for of course *Lady Hope* did not simply have a cook, next brought in desserts.

Hope clapped her hands, the sweets were so adorable. Huge chocolate-dipped strawberries, with V-shaped centers of white chocolate. Dotted on the white V were three tiny, dark-chocolate buttons and a bow tie.

"The strawberries are wearing tuxedos! That's wonderful," said Hope. "I love that."

The captain looked in briefly. He too was cranberry pink from too much sun and wind. His clothes were ice white with thin gold trim, and his sunglasses actually matched: gold rimmed. The crew was dressed entirely in white and gold. Hope was entranced. They were like boxed dolls, that came in a set on your birthday.

Each pillow on the built-in sofas was embroidered in delicate gold script with the same lovely name: *Lady Hope.* The frosted glass on the teak doors was etched with a profile of some ancient ship at sea, sails full and proud.

"You must love this boat," Hope said to the captain.

He smiled at her. "She's my life," he agreed. "She's a good girl. She's easy to clean, she's great-looking, her engines are in great shape. She was built strong enough to cross the Atlantic, and she's done it more than once, but she's a little too old to try it now. She winters in Fort Lauderdale."

Hope loved how he referred to the boat. He seemed to be talking of a beloved aunt or grandmother. His eyes rested with great affection on every inch of *Lady Hope.* Mr. Senneth seemed only to be passing through, as he passed through The Jayquith, but the captain lived on the boat, and loved her.

Hope had never thought much of people who loved inanimate objects. How could you *love* a car or a truck? But she could see that the crew loved *Lady Hope,* and somehow, moving gently in the rising tide, tugging on her ropes, *Lady Hope* did not seem inanimate. She seemed a living lady, with power and strength and beauty of her own.

"I hope I get to sail on her," said Hope, staring out the windows into the sun. The bay was impossibly beautiful, as if a net of gold had been drawn over it.

"You've sailed on her many times," said her father quietly.

The captain and chef exchanged looks and withdrew.

"Hope," said her father, "I'm going to level with you."

He took her hands in his and examined them, lightly stroking each finger with his thumbs, in a cool doctor-like way. As if she had arthritis and he wanted to heal it with touch. "I want you to tell me the truth, too," he said. He looked into her eyes now, his searching look just like his searching fingers: cool and careful and loving.

Hope burst into tears.

"I know that you can do tears on demand," he said, still gently. "You're very good with tears. But tears are not going to help you now."

Kaytha giggled.

She continued to fondle the ivory comb. She pressed her thumb down, and the comb clicked, metallically, and opened and closed.

It was not a comb.

It was a knife.

* * *

When it came to girls, Mitch had trouble with detail.

The girl he had taken to his high school senior prom was typical. One week prior to the prom, he bought her a beautiful pair of earrings.

"We've been dating for six months," she said dangerously, "and you haven't noticed that I do not have pierced ears?"

Mitch looked at her earlobes. Untouched by holes. "Oh," he said. "I thought everybody had pierced ears."

"Oh," she mimicked him, "and are you dating everybody? Or just me?"

"Well," said Mitch, trying to redeem himself. "We could go get them pierced."

"If I wanted them pierced, I'd have done it by now, wouldn't I?" said his girlfriend, smacking the earrings down in his palm hard enough to pierce his hand. And breaking one, so he couldn't even return them to the department store. "Furthermore," she said, "that isn't even real silver, Mitchell."

You knew you were in trouble when they called you Mitchell. The senior prom was more a night to forget than a night to remember.

Detail-wise, girls had continued to be a problem.

Boats, however, were easy. Mitch always knew and always remembered the details of boats.

Starry Night, old girl, thought Mitch, I need to check you out.

Every few weekends, Mitch went home for R & R. College was very wearing and a person liked to be waited on. Mitch's parents were among the few he knew who had never even contemplated divorce, who adored each other, whose hobbies matched, and whose interests jelled. Mitch's departure for college made his parents happy. Now they could spend time together undiluted by a son. Mitch, as he always explained, came home to get in the way. Remind them they were parents as well as boyfriend and girlfriend. Yeah, yeah, his father would say, tousling his hair as if he were six years old, well, I have a date with your mother, so make yourself scarce.

The family had sailed *Starry Night* for years — trips to Bermuda, the Florida Keys, islands off the coasts of Maine and Canada. Once they had crossed the ocean, although that had been a little hairy, because she was big sitting in port, but very, very little riding ocean waves.

Then one day they lost interest, didn't want

a captain and a steward, a first mate and an engineer and a chef. They bought a much smaller sailboat that they could manage between the two of them, and took up racing at the Yacht Club.

Mitch missed *Starry Night*.

I'll buy her back, he thought. I'll call her *Starry Night* again, because that's the kind of night Hope and I will have. It'll always be clear, and the stars will always shine.

Mitch never talked this way to anybody.

People, especially boys, would laugh hysterically.

He knew that Hope would not laugh. She would love.

He phoned home. "Dad? Listen. Who bought *Starry Night*?"

"I thought you only phoned home when you needed money," said his father.

"I'm rich. I sold a billion T-shirts this weekend. No. I called home because I need to know who bought *Starry Night*."

"We sold her to a corporation. We never met the buyers and I don't even know if there are individuals involved. Why?"

"I think," said Mitch, "that she's docked right here on Long Wharf in Boston. Her name's been changed. I'm not a hundred percent sure, Dad. But I'm ninety-nine."

"Just go aboard and ask," said his father. "Crews are always friendly. It probably has some of the same crew."

"No. Crew's all different. Paint's different. Decor's different."

"I don't want to hear another word," said his father. "I want to remember *Starry Night* exactly as she was."

"Would you look it up for me?" said Mitch.

"I wouldn't know where to start."

"Dad. You have a staff. Assign it to somebody."

"Is it urgent?" said his father, sighing.

"No, it's not urgent," said Mitch.

But he was wrong.

The glass slipped in Hope's hand.

She had designed a daydream, but it had turned on her. The action characters she had sketched now lived, and had muscles, and tense jaws and angry eyes.

"Tell me," said Kender Senneth, "what happened to your purse."

She choked on her own air. "I don't know who I am. Maybe I'm not Hope Senneth. Maybe I'm Susan Nevilleson. I can't be both. I want answers, too. But I don't have any. I think maybe I should go to the police."

She had meant to phone the police when

Mitch and Kaytha were on the swan boat, and been equally glad and sorry to be interrupted. Now she was wholly sorry.

"I think maybe you should sit here and tell me what is going on," said Mr. Senneth.

The room changed.

He was still distinguished and elegant, but full of rage and fear.

Kaytha had become the snake of her skull.

"Start with morning," said Mr. Senneth. "What did you do yesterday morning?"

"I don't remember."

"Tell us where you were before we found you."

"But I don't know!"

"It doesn't matter anyway. All that matters is your purse."

She held up her flat hands, as if using sign language would help. Shook her wrists, to show emptiness.

"Where did you put your purse?" Mr. Senneth was not breathing. Not blinking. He was a statue, a computer screen.

The smile on Kaytha's lips was as thin and sharp as a razor blade.

Chapter 9

Even though it was Saturday, and prime tourist time for hours to come, Mitch had closed up the T-shirt wagon and gone back to his apartment. He had to change his clothes, he said.

Derry sat on a bench with Ben Franklin. "Listen up. Susan is on board *Lady Hope.*"

"You're kidding! Oh, thank god. She did get a new job. I can stop worrying." Then he worried again. "Did she take your job, Derry? Gee, I'm sorry about that," said Ben, but already he was thinking about how terrific Susan would be as a yacht hostess, and what fun he would have visiting on board when the Senneths were out of town, and how he would definitely want to strip down and get in the upper deck jacuzzi with her, and —

"The hot dog seller saw Susan carried aboard *Lady Hope*. She was drunk."

"She was not," said Ben indignantly. "She — "

"Of course she wasn't," said Derry, leaning forward. "I totally agree with you, Ben. They forced her aboard."

All these melodramatic people. Half the world was acting out some play. He was even beginning to feel normal in a beard and granny glasses and wool waistcoat. "I thought you just said she took your job."

"*You* said that. I know better. They can't have a stranger on board."

"Why not?" said Ben. "Besides, if they took her on board, then they can and do have a stranger on board."

Derry was wearing bib front, shoulder-strapped overalls. Her figure was entirely gone. She'd fastened her hair in a topknot high on her head and jammed a Red Sox cap down over it. The bill of the cap was sagging, the dye faded. She was difficult to recognize as the white-and-gold stewardess with the puppy attitude. She had changed personalities like . . .

Like a spy, thought Ben Franklin. This nonsense is infecting even me. I suppose everybody has spy fantasies. Of course, all the good countries are gone now. Either they're submerged in submachine guns and disease, or nobody cares about them anymore. You're stuck with industrial spying, worrying about people's computer chips.

"You're boarding the boat, Ben, and taking Susan off," said Derry firmly. "I can't crash the party, because they know me. But you can."

You, too, can be a spy, thought Ben Franklin. You too can crash parties and whisk unwilling girls off in your arms. He said, "Derry, Susan didn't even let me telephone her, never mind take her off a yacht the first time in her life she's ever been on one."

"Trust me," said Derry, as if he knew her, as if he had the slightest idea whether she was trustworthy. "I know these people. They are not people of violence. All you have to do is board the boat, find Susan, and leave. Now here's the layout of the boat. She has to be in my bunk, because there's no place else to stash her."

"What do you mean, *stash?*"

"I told you, she's their prisoner."

Even though Ben had been frantically worried all day that something terrible had happened to Susan, now that Derry was describing it, he knew it was absolutely ridiculous. This was Boston. Nobody had been taken prisoner here in hundreds of years.

"How could they keep her quiet?" said Ben skeptically. "Susan has lungs."

"I'll bet she does. They could have drugged her, or gagged her, or be sitting there with a knife."

"Derry, I can't believe," said Ben Franklin, "that that beautiful boat is manned by people who kidnap waitresses. I mean, what's the point? There has to be a purpose."

Derry paid no attention to him. This happened a lot to Ben Franklin. "Mr. Senneth entertains a great deal on *Lady Hope.* He's one of the finer con artists I've ever seen. He can't allow anything to go wrong at this stage."

"This stage of what?" said Ben Franklin.

"Everyone coming tonight will be very, very rich, and very very influential. That's the only kind of person he cultivates. And people love being invited aboard yachts. They'll have some fabulous dinner on board, probably take a brief sunset sail, and then drink the night away. He can't change his plans just because he's taken prisoners."

"Taken prisoners," muttered Ben Franklin. "That's ludicrous."

"You'll look wonderful in a tux," said Derry. "Nobody will confuse you with Ben Franklin. You're handsome and debonair."

"Me?" said Ben Franklin.

"You. In a tuxedo, you know, you're so solid and successful. Thin doesn't make it in men's evening clothes; thin looks like a weakling. You're stocky and broad, Ben, and anybody can tell you have millions of dollars and a great deal of influence."

Ben liked that. "What if they catch on to what I'm doing before I find Susan?"

"They won't. They have a boatful of guests. This is a big important party because he's involved in a big important event. You're going to circulate. They always do tours, because people love to see a big yacht. But they'll leave out crew quarters, which is where Susan has to be. I know everyone on the crew and I'll describe them to you, so you'll quickly figure out if any crew member is not showing up, and then you'll know that crew member is probably guarding Susan. But my guess is, Susan is just tied up in there."

Ben could absolutely not imagine Susan, tough little Susan, allowing anybody to immobilize her.

"But even if she is tied up, and even if I manage to untie her," said Ben Franklin, "what happens when we go through the salon? Cross the deck? It's a big boat, but it's not the *QE II*. The Senneths will notice."

"Mr. Senneth absolutely *cannot* have a fracas during his gala event. He can't have people issuing death threats or yanking out weapons or chasing his passengers. So when you find Susan, you just saunter out with her on your arm and leave the boat."

Ben could see some real problems here. Like, what if this was not what Susan had in mind? "What if I crash the party," he said, "and Susan's right there, serving drinks, or something, and she's absolutely fine?"

Derry shrugged and smiled. "Then I was nuts, and you're on board a magnificent yacht during the party of the year with the girl you adore."

Ben had a vision of himself as hero: the kind of role Mitch always got, while he, Ben, was the buffoon, the sidekick, the comic. Do you learn to be a hero, he wondered, or are you born one?

"I tell you, these are not violent people. Just greedy. They can't risk their cover for you or for Susan."

Derry made it easy and even logical. As if he ought to do this.

What he ought to do, he knew perfectly well, was sit down and think.

If Susan mattered so little that he could wander in and wander off with her, why kidnap her in the first place? What had ever made such an idea cross Derry's mind in the second place? Had she witnessed such things when she crewed? And if Susan was in danger, and Derry knew it, why not just call the police?

"Why not just call the police?" said Ben, but even as he said it he had a hideous vision of Susan letting him know what she thought of him, interfering with her job selection by calling in the Boston police force!

"You'll look so suave in evening clothes," coaxed Derry.

He wanted to be coaxed. If it was a con, he wanted to be conned. Everyone, everywhere, wants to be the hero, the dashing one in the best clothes, who saves the day.

He did not wonder if, instead, he might lose the day.

Or his life.

"I am older than my cousin," explained Edie, in the voice of one telling a cozy bedtime story, "and we did not grow up together. I spent much of my life in boarding schools in Switzerland, of course, and our paths rarely crossed. The occasional holiday only."

Susan marveled at how Edie said, *in Switzerland, of course*. "Of course," she said, just to fit in.

"I had no idea how Uncle Ken maintained

his wealth," said Edie. "I suppose I foolishly thought he had excellent investments. Well, of course, he did. It was just that the investments did not belong to him."

The bunks were very close, the quarters incredibly cramped. How did you make such a bed? Where did you get the sheets and how did you tuck them?

But being close had a distinct advantage: Edie, whose feet were free, had stuck out a foot and with her long curly toes managed to open the little curtain that kept Susan in the dark.

Susan stared at the woman. T-shirt, platinum-dyed hair that either Edie had planned to let go back to brunette or had missed the last ten hair appointments for, shorts, and bare feet with remarkably long toes. They were so unlike Susan's little stubby toes (all of me is stubby, thought Susan with her usual regret) they didn't seem like the same part of the anatomy.

"I," said Edie, "was brought to America as a tutor for Kaytha. She can't go to school because her jealousy turns violent, and she likes knives."

Oh, wonderful, thought Susan. And I suppose it seemed reasonable to live with Kaytha after you found that out? Did you say to yourself, Ah, at last! My dream job! "Peachy," muttered Susan. Who is going to rescue me? she thought desperately. They made me telephone Michael and say I was quitting. Michael believed me. There was no way to let him know he should worry. He won't call Mitch or Ben Franklin and say, we've got to find Susan and rescue her. He'll just be furious and instead of searching for me, he'll be replacing me.

Edie said, "The Senneths have tremendous wealth. Actually, they use other people's wealth. The very, very rich are also very, very careless. Very easy to use. Kender Senneth is a brilliant con artist. There's something terribly attractive about fabulous wealth, you know, Susan. A person wants some of it for herself."

Susan was trying to stay calm, but a person tied up on a boat, after being kidnapped at knife-point does not manage to stay calm. She thought, I do not care about money. I do not care about the Senneths' appealing lifestyle. I just want to go home and stay alive. I have to plan our escape.

"Where are we?" Susan asked. "I mean, within the boat? Whose bunks are these?"

"Crew. The staterooms are magnificent. They aren't wasting those on us. A little puppy of a girl, named Derry, was bunked in yours, and I'm in Billy's. The big event occurred on little Derry's day off. When she got back, what with her bunk filled by me, they had to fire her. She's dumb. She won't suspect anything. She won't go to the police, if that's what you're thinking, and save us."

Susan tried to think who would save them, but no list came to mind.

Susan had yanked at the plastic handcuffs that attached her to the brass fittings around the bunk enough times to leave her wrists raw and painful. "But why me?" she said. "I still can't understand what I have to offer them, or how I fit into anything."

"You're Susan Nevilleson."

"So what?" cried Susan. "How would they know me? Kaytha did have lunch a few times in the restaurant, and I remember thinking I would never ever give myself a crewcut, never mind carve snakes in it afterward, but what's the point in kidnapping me?"

"You're Susan Nevilleson."

They're all insane, thought Susan. Edie's just as crazy as Kaytha, she just hasn't shaved her head yet.

"Your Cousin Edie," said Mr. Senneth, giving it one more try, "took a beautiful piece of family history. A magnificent necklace that belonged to your mother, and her mother before her, and her mother before that."

He is seducing me, she thought, not through sex, but through wealth. Their way of life is beckoning to me. Their money is greeting me.

"You were to be the fourth generation to wear it, Hope." He was stricken by the loss, aching to see Hope wearing the beautiful piece of family history.

"I don't remember," she whispered.

"But you must at least remember the necklace itself! The thick gold chain? The heavy emeralds and diamonds? Slabs, almost. Immense stones. The necklace was a queen's ransom."

"I don't remember."

"You could not forget the necklace," said Kender Senneth. "You used to love wearing it. We let you wear it for a few minutes at a time on special occasions."

She wanted to believe him. He was such a nice man, so distinguished. She wanted to agree to bring him the necklace.

"I don't remember," she had said. Over and over. How could they argue with that? And she could never contradict herself.

"We must have the necklace back, Hope. We've taken immense loans out against it. The necklace belongs to the bank more than to us, and we must have it."

She could see no way, now, to tell the truth. She could not risk admitting what had really happened to that necklace after it fell to the bottom of her linen drawstring bag.

If he's telling the truth, thought Hope, although truth seemed to be in very short supply, and if I tell the truth, too — I'll go to jail! I'll be the one who's done terrible things. So I'll stay with my two safe sentences: I don't know. I don't remember.

"Edie wanted to sell it to support her drug habit," he said.

"Edie?" she repeated.

"Another cousin," whispered Kaytha. "The ship is full of them."

Hope shivered. Mr. Senneth had made Kaytha put the knife away. He was so casual about it, you would have thought Hope had been right the first time, and the ivory container held a comb.

The ship is full of them. She had a vision of little cousins, scrabbling around like rats in the hold. "I don't remember," she said again, trying to hold onto that. That she did not remember.

"I believe her," said Kaytha finally. "She doesn't know. She doesn't remember." Kaytha turned to leave the salon, and the forked tongue of the carved snake seemed to smile at Hope from the back of Kaytha's skull. Kaytha had double faces, as unmatched as her head and body.

But when Kaytha left from boredom, claiming she had more interesting things to do, Mr. Senneth continued interrogating from — what? What emotion pulled him on?

His voice was smooth and flat, like the sea without wind. And like the sea, it had depths and currents of which she knew nothing. He ignored Billy when he came into the room.

"You probably did see that shooting," said Mr. Senneth, "and I suppose I could believe you're blocking it out. Blocking out the moment in which Edie gave you the necklace. After all, there's a certain similarity between the events." He was trembling now, approaching some sort of emotional cliff.

"Ken," said Billy quietly. "Back off. The past won't help. It has nothing to do with her."

"It has everything to do with her," said Mr. Senneth.

He hates me, thought Hope. Kender Senneth hates me. How can he hate a person who does not exist? What nightmares have I tumbled into?

She had thought Mr. Senneth so kind and

thoughtful, so courteous and distinguished, so articulate and urbane. He continued to be some of those: he remained distinguished and urbane and articulate. But the kind, the thoughtful, and the courteous were eaten away as if by rust and the sea.

Hope began shivering uncontrollably, just when the thing she most needed was control. "You're asking all the questions," she said, playing for time and understanding. "It's time I asked a few."

"You?" said Mr. Senneth. "Your job is to answer, not to ask."

"Why do you hate me?"

Billy sucked in his breath and blew it out. "No, Kender, don't discuss that," said Billy, his voice nothing like a servant's. His voice a commander's. "This won't help us. We need answers, not a verbal whipping."

Hope recognized him at last. The all too healthy-looking homeless man who had sat down on the bench beside her. When had that been? It felt like weeks before. It had been yesterday. And he had sat there — she had thought at the time — to rob her; to take her purse.

That's what he did, she thought suddenly. That was his purpose. To take my purse. But of course I didn't have it anymore. So instead . . .

"Who shot at you, though?" said Susan. "Everybody heard a shot."

"Kender did. My own uncle. He didn't actually aim at me, of course, he just wanted me to know he was serious."

Nice family, thought Susan.

"I thought," said Edie, "that since this was my uncle, my very own blood relative, he'd surrender to the circumstances. He'd say, Oh, well, you win some, you lose some. He'd give up on the Queen Isabella idea, and we'd go our separate ways, because obviously we can't work well together, and that would be that."

"No, huh?" Questioning Edie was like questioning a three-year-old. You kept getting answers you didn't care about, and having to be sweet, and offer a candy bar.

"No," said Edie. "Aside from the fact that he invested a great deal of time and money in this plan, Kender seems to feel that I will contact the authorities and discuss his past, present, and future and he will be ruined. You see, Kender makes a market in stolen art. He's very clever. He's pulled off thefts from the Louvre and the British Museum and the Metropolitan in New York City. Kender is a very elegant man, very distinguished, very, very wealthy. He frequents these circles. In fact, he is on the Board of Trustees of the Metropolitan Museum. Kender helped arrange for the Queen Isabella necklace to be taken to Portugal for a year on an art exchange. Of course, he also arranged to substitute a paste necklace for the real one. He has a buyer. There are always people willing to buy great works of art, stolen or not, and this necklace is a great work of art. They'll get millions and millions for those stones."

Susan did not care about millions and millions. She cared about the span of her own life.

"Let's tell him you'd never turn him in," said Susan, who was happy to bargain. Mr. Senneth was welcome to his future, as long as Susan could have one, too. "He wouldn't actually hurt you, would he? His own niece?"

"No, no, Kaytha will do it. Kender is not a violent man. Kaytha, however, is a violent woman."

Wonderful. Susan tested the plastic handcuffs again. They looked so fragile, like a cheap Halloween trick for a six-year-old. But the handcuffs were going to work for just as long as the owner of the keys wanted them to.

Kaytha was the owner of the keys.

"Her father is not happy with her tendency to hurt people," said Edie. "He knows he should have had her locked up long ago, but he can't face the explanations he'd have to make in order to do it."

"What explanations would he have to make?"

"He'd have to start with what Kaytha has done in the past. He'd have to move on to what she did to her last roommate in her last boarding school. Very expensive payoff, that one. He'd have to end with — "

"Enough," said Susan. She didn't want to know what Kaytha had done. Perhaps waitressing wasn't so bad. There were worse things than grubby tourists. Boat-bottom prisons were one. Sea bottoms were another.

She struggled with the chaotic story Edie was telling, the pieces that went here, and the parts that went there. She still could not figure out how she, Susan Nevilleson, fit into this.

"I could not go along with them," said Edie, rather prissily. "I wasn't brought up that way. It seemed easy enough to ruin their little necklace scheme: I'd take the copy and toss it in some Dumpster. Unfortunately, my timing was off."

Most things about Edie appeared to be off.

The bigger surprise was that the Senneths allowed Edie to be close to any of this at all. But peculiar relatives plagued every family. Although the Senneth family seemed to be nothing but peculiar relatives.

"Kender and Billy flung me back into the limousine. They hadn't seen me drop the jewelry into the open purse of that girl on the sidewalk. They thought I'd stashed it somewhere in the hotel, or the parking garage, or somebody else's car. And of course they had to find out where it was. They are going to do a quick substitution that nobody will suspect. So they have to have the fake necklace. And they have to have it on Tuesday, when the switch is arranged."

Susan made a considerable effort to arrange freedom for herself, but there was absolutely no way to get those plastic handcuffs off. Her short stature had not, unfortunately, given her starvation-thin wrists. She could not suddenly slenderize them and yank herself back out of the handcuffs.

The necklace that all the fuss was about then, was not the real necklace. The real necklace was still in the museum. I've been kidnapped, she thought, to protect a fake.

And what else was fake?

Miss Amnesia? Was she fake? But why? For

all the answers Edie was dealing her, Susan still understood nothing.

"But Kaytha was in The Jayquith watching from the seventh floor, where actually, of course, for that price you get a fabulous view, and Kaytha saw the whole thing. She could identify the girl into whose bag I had dropped the necklace. Of course nobody thought they'd ever see the necklace again. They were all *stunned* when the girl reappeared a few hours later. Just wandered out onto the plaza like a lost kitten waiting to be adopted."

That's exactly how she looked, thought Susan. Miss Amnesia was a lost kitten. The most beautiful kitten in the world, waiting to be adopted.

Edie smiled a crazy smile at the low ceiling above her bunk. "Or drowned," she added.

Susan did not like hearing the word *drowned* when she herself was prisoner on an ocean-going vessel.

Susan wanted to be prepared. If by any remote chance she was able to free herself, she wanted to have her next moves in mind. "Can we make a getaway on the Wave Runners?" Susan asked Edie seriously.

"I doubt it. They're three stories above the water, remember. You can't just throw them off. You've got to hook them onto the davit, and wind it up, and direct it up and over the rails and out over the water, and then unwind them down into the water. It's very time-consuming." Edie returned to the subject of acting. "Now, Kaytha loves drama. She is a very dramatic person herself, you know." Edie paused. "Killers are."

Susan lost her grip. "How can you be so relaxed about this?" she screamed. "Kaytha may slit our throats and weight our ankles with cement and lower us overboard and you just lie there and discuss it like overdue library books?"

Edie was twitching up and down the whole length of her body. "To Kaytha," said Edie, "we *are* nothing but used library books. Once we are no further use to her, she'll toy with us for a while, but then she'll get bored. Or it will get too messy. She's really quite fastidious so it won't last as long as it would if she liked blood."

"But why *my* blood?" cried Susan. "What does Kaytha think *I* can do for her?"

"You told her you knew about the necklace."

"Well, I do," said Susan. "It was in the newspapers. It's a big diplomatic deal. People are saying the Queen Isabella necklace really belongs to Portugal anyway. It's an interesting argument, who owns what in antiquities." She was beginning to sound like Edie, blathering away on useless side issues. The point was to get away from here. Who cared if she understood what was going on?

"People are easy for Kender to fool," said Edie, rather proudly. "He's so dignified and attractive. You want him to be in charge, because he's so civilized. Kender really is a brilliant actor. It's a shame he never went on stage. Of course, there's so much more money in what he really does."

"How much money?" said Susan.

"I think they expect about ten million for the necklace. If you hadn't said you knew about the necklace, Kaytha wouldn't have misunderstood. She thought you were Susan Nevilleson, and she could make you give it to her. So Kaytha stuck a knife in your side, and she and Billy brought you here to get the information out of you."

"I *am* Susan Nevilleson," said Susan. "Though why that is such a key point, I cannot imagine."

"Her boyfriend was looking for her," explained Edie, as if Susan Nevilleson was somebody else entirely, and not strapped to the bunk next to her.

Susan Nevilleson's boyfriend? thought Susan Nevilleson.

"He asked that gorgeous T-shirt seller if he'd seen her, and of course, the T-shirt kid had. Obviously Miss Amnesia had something to do with, or was, Susan Nevilleson. Naturally Kaytha and Billy looked Susan Nevilleson up in the phone book and went to see if she had gone home after she cracked her head on the sidewalk and left the necklace there where they could just retrieve it."

Mitch McKenna, you did this to me! You put me here. You couldn't make up a name for your script, oh no. You couldn't say the non-existent boyfriend was looking for Gwendolyn Carlough-Simms, oh no. You had to use a real girl's real name. Mine. You rotten egg, Mitch McKenna. I hate you.

She really did.

She was furious with him — carrying his acting into real life. Acting belonged on stage — that was why they built stages! That was why they had films and movies! For acting!

Ben Franklin wouldn't have been a jerk like that! she thought. He wouldn't drag me into something that could mean my very own death! He —

The door was opening.

Whoever came in could only be the person who had brought Susan here to start with. Kaytha of the knife.

Mitch, Mitch, how could you have put me in this position? And how will I ever get out?

Chapter 10

She twisted her bronze hair in her hands, to give herself something to do as she stared at Mr. Senneth. Beautiful though it was, it was remarkably thick, as if like the hull of *Lady Hope*, it had extra coats of polish. As she, herself, at this moment, was coated in layers of falsehoods.

For she knew exactly who she was. She had known every moment. And she was not Hope Senneth.

How had she gotten here? And how, at this point, was she going to get out safely?

Her mother and father, ordinary unsophisticated people, wanted her to be just like them: living in the same small town, being just as dull and ordinary. They kept saying that every high school girl who'd ever had the lead in her high school play was convinced she had a future on stage. It didn't mean a thing, they kept saying, that the local paper gave her rave reviews. It wouldn't count in New York.

"Then let me go to New York!" she cried out. "Let me find out if I can really act!"

They wouldn't let her apply to drama school and, as for New York City, they regarded that as the most dangerous terrifying grim place on earth. Not only did they refuse to let her go to college in New York, they didn't even want her to get on a train that went *through* New York!

You have to go to New York to be an actress! their daughter cried, sobbing and blackmailing and pleading and coaxing.

You're not going to be an actress and you're not going to New York and that's that, was the answer.

What they finally agreed to, was letting their darling girl interview at little New England colleges. Sweet isolated campuses studded with stone walls and maple trees.

She didn't get off the train in New York. She didn't even really *see* New York; the train was mean and unfair and stayed underground for the good parts. And then the train stopped in Boston. And Boston, too, was a city. A real city. Filled with colleges. It occurred to her that she could get accepted at a college in Boston, get accepted there, act there, and surely in a semester, or even a week, prove herself to be New York material. She would tell her parents about the old historic houses and somehow convince them that Boston was a dear little city with no threats.

She wandered the streets of Boston, with half a day to kill before her first interview, daydreaming of cities, and city women, and city life, and city money, and most of all city theater — when Edie happened. She fell backward, and cars missed her, although they did take time out to roll down their windows, let all their air-conditioning out, and swear at her. She hit her head, cracked her elbow, and felt equal parts a fool and a target. She ran ten blocks before her lungs and her calves hurt so much she had to stop. And there, in her bag, was the exotic, incredibly heavy, ridiculously bejeweled necklace.

It was like being handed half a script. The most intriguing improv class a high school girl ever had! Immediately she wanted to go back to that fabulous rich-people hotel, The Jayquith, from whose underground parking the limousine had crept, and meet society people and gangsters. The part of her that was sane knew perfectly well that nothing would happen at all, let alone anything exciting or wonderful or crazy. Far from proving to her mother and father that she really was the world's greatest actress, she'd just end up standing around on the pavement while the traffic ignored her just as much as it had the first time. Heck, the first time, she hadn't even figured out how to cross the street! So she knew that although it was a dumb idea, it was also a safe idea, because nothing would happen. It was just a silly girl's silly way to spend an hour.

She had the advantage of her beauty — or what, in a small town, people claimed was beauty. Perhaps it was like acting: She was lovely only as long as the competition was limited. But at home, people did things for her that they didn't bother to do for other women. She was sure that she could talk her way into the hotel.

It was a minor blow to her ego when the doorman wouldn't let her near it, let alone in it. Who was she visiting? he said. She made up a name, thinking that there must be far too many people in The Jayquith for him to recognize one from another, but it turned out that tourists were always trying to use The Jayquith like McDonald's, for the bathroom, and he turned her away.

Now what? Here she was all ready to be a

fabulous actress and nobody would allow her on stage. Nobody would do their half of the script.

The thought came to her, as she took heavy disappointed steps, that she was anonymous. In a small town, attending a small high school, you are never anonymous. You are always known.

Why not be *really* anonymous? After all, she had seen something very shocking and also hit her head. Why not pretend to be anonymous even to herself? Why not have amnesia! And if she made a fool of herself, who would ever know? Only strangers she would never see again.

She had walked around the other side of The Jayquith, following the crowds, turning herself into a terrified confused girl with amnesia. It was a wonderful part. She let go of all her thoughts. She called upon fear and terror to occupy her mind, because if you really forgot yourself, think how terrified you would be! she thought. She went way beyond thinking, right into terror. She had never acted terror before, and she found out she could scare herself so much her hair really did prickle and her heart really did beat faster and her breath really did grow shallow.

She moved out of her previous life. She

abandoned thinking and knowledge and remembrance. She drew herself out of her mind until she really was so confused and afraid that she really did need to be rescued. Her head truly ached and her thoughts truly became mist and cloud.

She would be the best amnesia victim there ever was, she said to herself. An Academy-Award-winning amnesia victim.

Nobody's brain damage is the same as anybody else's brain damage, so any symptoms were her call. And did she ever call them up! She loved being woozy and confused and vulnerable and weak. She loved not remembering some things but having to remember others.

She was not just the actress, she was the producer, the writer, the camera, and the audience.

She had hardly even started when the handsomest young man in New England — the lover in any girl's script — walked right up. He really did make her woozy. Her heart lurched when somebody in the crowd suggested calling the police. What would her mother and father say to that! She truly thought she would faint, and she had an extra good reason to cling to Mitch: Just imagine what her parents would say about this little acting job.

Stop this, she had said to herself at that moment. Laugh it off, walk away, abandon this stupid, stupid idea, which is only going to cause trouble.

. . . when up came a parent.

A serious dignified man . . . who claimed to be her father.

There wasn't time to say to herself: *Wait.* You aren't this man's daughter. He knows that. He's acting too. There's something radically wrong — *get away; give it up.* If there'd been time to sit and think about it, perhaps she would have fled to the train station, gone on to the sweet little campuses. But for better or worse, she was given no space in which to contemplate it.

It was meant, she let herself believe. There is another half to the script. I can't pass it up.

She would be the one person to find out if she really could step into another person's life. Everybody's television fantasy. Could she pull it off, with no mistakes and no missteps?

She who had always wanted a magnificent radiant trembling secret that everybody would be jealous of, if they knew. A secret on every level, from every person.

And in The Jayquith! The incredible wealth and splendor of that place came complete with a cousin who knew her and dinner that was ordered for her. Even a perfect name. Hope. She had been acting confused, but now there was no need to act. What on earth was going on? Who could these people be? What on earth was their motive?

And what is my motive? she thought. Why am I going on with this? I've got to run, not tuck myself into this like a person lying under blankets.

And then . . . *they produced a passport of her.*

She hadn't had anything to eat that day. She was light-headed. And suddenly, her skit turned inside out like a sweater, with seams and threads on the wrong side. How deeply could you fall into a role? How intensely could you play a part? Could you actually, on the portable stage of the world, *become that person?*

Who was the act?

Was she really Hope? A girl she did not remember — *but they did?*

A passport.

The accepted proof the world around.

She'd gotten so deeply into her act, she couldn't be sure where the edge of the stage was, and where real life began. Hope — or not Hope? Was she the best actress in the world, or had she fallen off the edge of sanity?

And whatever the answers — who were these people? These Senneths?

And then there was Mitch. Like a storybook prince, he had arrived just to fall in love, as if that were his only role on stage: to kneel beside the sleeping princess and kiss her lips and awaken her. But when they all awakened — when the truth was revealed — Mitch would find he had fallen in love with a person who did not exist at all. Perhaps had never existed, in spite of the passport.

The kicker in this was that Mitch loved her for her mystery, and for her status and position and wealth. What was he going to say when he found she was the dullest of girls from the dullest of towns?

She needed all kinds of time, and lengthy phone calls to exchange thinking with her girlfriends, and perhaps a chocolate sundae, in order to see things clearly.

Instead she had Kaytha and a terribly angry man, to whom a real Hope had done something awful. She saw now that Kender Senneth's script called for revenge. He, too, needed an actress: somebody to play Hope. Somebody to lash out at and punish.

And that punishment . . . what would it be? For it would be real. Amnesia could be faked, and trembling and confusion could be falsified, but the punishment that Mr. Senneth had in mind would actually exist.

"You and I are returning to The Jayquith," said Mr. Senneth at last. In her wildly active imagination, it sounded as if they were returning to the guillotine.

She swallowed. The flashbacks in her head stopped. She had wasted precious time, when she could have been planning an escape.

"The party we have planned for tonight is far too important for you to ruin," said Mr. Senneth, just like a parent. "You'll be in the suite at the hotel during the party. Very, very sound asleep."

She thought: We have both fallen into our roles completely. He thinks I am his daughter. But who is Hope? And how do I stop being her without getting hurt in the process?

Mr. Senneth took out a small dark plastic bottle; a prescription bottle. "This is Dr. Patel's newest attempt at calming you down," he said. "Take six of these."

She backed up against the salon wall, pressed against the maps of treacherous waters. Six of anything was too much. She couldn't take some unknown medication at all — and certainly not six.

He handed her her own glass of bubbly water to swallow the pills with.

She burst into tears, which had worked before. But it did not work for her now. Billy held her arms, and Mr. Senneth tilted her head, as if she were a cat and they were veterinarians, and they poured the pills and the water down her throat.

The hotel staff saw nothing but a lovely girl, with her father and a friend on either side of her, the men laughing and talking as they walked her into a side door at The Jayquith, and quickly entered the private elevator.

"So you carved your little snake design into your hair with your own pocket knife?" said Susan.

Susan did not learn quickly. She never had. "You're a total idiot, you know, Kaytha. People have seen you all over the place, and they've seen this boat, and they're going to know where you come from."

She could not believe the little squirrely smile on Kaytha's face either: as if Kaytha were tucking Susan's hurt and fear into her cheeks to chew on later.

Edie said, "Susan, what we need to do, you and I, is play whatever game Kaytha wants to play."

"It isn't a game," said Kaytha. "It's real,

Cousin Edie. It was a real necklace and you're going to die a real death."

"It was *not* a real necklace!" cried Edie. "That's the point, Kaytha."

Mr. Senneth came in and Kaytha flicked the knife shut. Now it was just a long elegant slightly curved object. It looked as if it could have had a clasp in back, to hold your ponytail. It looked like ivory.

Made from an endangered creature, thought Susan. Like me. I am an endangered creature right now.

"Kaytha," said Mr. Senneth, "we agreed we're not going to do that kind of thing again."

"I never agree with you on anything," said Kaytha. "I didn't agree this time either."

"Leave them alone. We have enough problems. I cannot believe you brought this woman Susan back to the boat. What are we supposed to do with her?" Mr. Senneth was not the distinguished gentleman that Susan had seen handling Miss Amnesia. He was frantic and trembling. He did not recognize her as the colonial-garbed waitress, she was sure.

"We had to get rid of Edie anyhow," said Kaytha. "We'll just get rid of both of them.

"Kaytha, we can't just get rid of them."

Susan was happy to hear it.

"If we don't get rid of them," Kaytha pointed

out, "they will go to the police and our lives as the Senneth family will end. You will not be sought after socially. You will not be on important boards of major museums and philanthropies. You will not dine with stockbrokers eager for your business. You will have no yacht, no Jayquith Hotel suite, no French country manor, no nothing. You will have prison. Toilets without seats in rooms with cockroaches, both human and insect."

Mr. Senneth made fists. There was hardly room to do that or anything else. The tiny space curved to a point, where Susan's and Edie's feet nearly met, the space between the bunks barely enough for one person to get dressed in. Kaytha and Mr. Senneth were inches and breaths away from each other.

"Kaytha," he said wearily, "this should have been so simple. I cannot believe we have hostages and death threats. All I wanted was ten million dollars."

All? thought Susan. He thinks that's minor?

"We've done so many museum switches," he said. "We've got fakes in museums all over Europe, and gotten away with it, and we never had to threaten a single person and we have never been in danger ourselves. And now look what you have done!"

"Blame me?" said Kaytha furiously. "It's

Edie who took the necklace! Blame her. I'm blaming her, even if you don't. I'm lowering her overboard, even if you don't. I might lower you overboard too, while I'm at it. You love having Hope for a daughter, don't you? She's just what you want in a daughter, isn't she? She's beautiful and stunning and graceful. She's smart and quick and athletic, and she eats all her meals and doesn't throw them up."

"Kaytha, stop it."

"That's all you ever say to me — stop it. Well, I'm your real daughter, Kender Senneth, and it's your turn to stop it! Stop pretending that beautiful girl is your little girl. Get rid of her. She's in the way."

"She knows where the necklace is! She's the one we have to interrogate, Kaytha, not this stranger."

"Then why did you take her back to the hotel? Why let her sleep all neat and clean and safe? Why not skip the party tonight, and sail out to sea, and let her watch what I do to these two, and then I bet she'll tell us where the necklace is."

Kaytha's hatred oozed out of her. Susan had never been so terrified in her life.

"You like pretending I'm your niece instead of your daughter, don't you?" shrieked Kaytha. "You're ashamed to have me for a daughter! You probably wouldn't mind if I went overboard and you got to keep Miss Amnesia!"

Susan tried to pull the emotional level down. "I'm a little confused," she said, with massive understatement. She wanted to know who Hope was. "Mitch said you had her passport. Mitch saw her photo on it. The girl is Hope Senneth."

Kaytha giggled, a sick hot chortle.

Mr. Senneth said, "Hope Senneth is dead. I don't know who the girl is."

Hope Senneth is dead, thought Susan. How did she die? Will I die like Hope Senneth? Just for a necklace?

Or is it just for acting? Because of Mitch, and his act? These people, and their act? Miss Amnesia, whoever she is, and her act?

"I'm not involved," said Susan. "I won't go to the police. I won't go to anybody. Just let me go, okay? I'll just run along home and forget the whole thing."

"That's a crock," said Kaytha.

Mr. Senneth rested his head in his hands. "I'm afraid it is a crock," he said, "vulgar term though that is. Of course you would go to the authorities. Please explain to me, rather than Kaytha forcing you to explain to me, who Mitch McKenna is, and why he is involved."

Kaytha played with her knife again and this time Mr. Senneth did not ask her to quit.

Susan directed a few hateful thoughts toward Mitch. "He's just a college kid," said Susan. "He fell head over heels in love with Miss Amnesia and he thought of a way to get up to your suite and make you prove to him that she is Hope Senneth. Mitch is an actor, we all are — drama majors — and he thought up a skit that might work, and he used my name. I don't have anything to do with this."

Kaytha smiled. "You do now."

"No, Kaytha," said her father wearily. "The guests will be arriving shortly. Go get dressed. Whatever else we do, we have to make this party work. Every one of these guests will be at the Museum on Tuesday, they will all have complete faith in me, and never worry while I am near the real necklace. And somehow I am still going to get the fake and do the switch and get my ten million."

He strapped Edie and Susan down, and even though he apologized for the pain and distress he knew it would cause, taped their mouths again. He didn't cover Susan's eyes.

After all, she couldn't yell to the party guests with her eyes.

* * *

Hope had proof now, that she was a solid actress.

She had let them walk her to the hotel, pretending to be completely out of the picture from the medication. Any thoughts she might have had about screaming for help were subdued by the fact that both Mr. Senneth and Billy were armed.

Then she played a perfect Sleep scene, only slightly less difficult than a Dead Body scene. She had acted asleep for fifteen long minutes. It had felt like a quarter of a century.

"She's out," said Mr. Senneth at last. "I don't have anyone to stay with her. Let's get back to the boat. I have to be there for the guests."

"Do we lock her in?" asked Billy. "I hate having her here on her own. Why couldn't we leave her on the boat?"

"There's a limit to the number of prisoners we can handle," said Mr. Senneth. He sounded very dangerously strung out. "Fifty guests are going to want to tour every inch of the yacht. We can keep them out of the crew room where Edie and the girl are, but where do we put this one? So we're here, and we made it, and somehow I'm going to get through the party and somehow I'm finding the necklace. There's no way to lock her in. Fire laws, you know. If she wakes up, she can get out. But she can't wake up, not with a double dose."

There were no departing footsteps. The carpeting in the suite muffled everything. She slept on in pretense. She heard a door shut.

I won't get up yet, she thought, I'll wait another quarter of an hour and be absolutely sure nobody stayed behind.

She faked on.

But this time, what with stress and fear, it was not an act. She was as deeply asleep as if she really had swallowed all six pills, and not held three of them beneath her tongue, letting them fall out as they forced her back down the ladder from the boat. Three pills had made no noise falling into the water, but just sloshed quietly away. The other three, however, were doing their job.

The collection of grown-up toys lay neatly wrapped in white canvas on the flat-topped deck. Tiny stainless steel stairs curved upward to reach it. It had a bar, and a wonderful arched white canopy with a lacy flapping trim. Fifty people could dance there. The band had arranged itself among the toys.

Wave Runners, Jet Skis, Boston Whaler to pull the water skis, Sunfish, scuba sets, snorkeling gear — anything a water-loving guest could want. Derry had explained that you hardly ever had a water-loving guest and they never wanted to touch the toys. But they loved knowing that the toys were there — that they *could* have used them.

There was no song this band could not play. Guests who were seventy, guests who were eighteen, guests who were forty-five, and guests who were thirty: the band played the hit tunes from any year in the 20th century.

People danced.

They laughed.

They admired the lovely graceful yacht and were thrilled to find that the captain would take them on a starlit sail in Boston Harbor.

The portly young man whose dinner jacket had purple velvet lapels — not atrocious, but crazy, so you had to laugh when you saw him; he was dashing and creative — entranced the older women. "And what did you say your name is?" asked a blue-haired old lady with whom he was waltzing.

"Ben Franklin," he said, forgetting which role went where.

"You poor thing. Were your parents demented? Do you have brothers named George Washington and Lafayette?"

Ben Franklin laughed easily. "For the summer I'm an employee of the Park Service. I spend the day wandering around being an historical personage to tourists. Naturally, everybody just calls me Ben Franklin."

The group was entertained.

There was nothing Ben Franklin loved more than a party, except being the center of attention at that party. He was having a wonderful time. All the possibilities he had frightened himself with were ridiculous. It was easy to blend in. Nobody wanted controversy, nobody wanted details — they just wanted a laugh, a drink, and a dance.

Ben was a wonderful dancer, which most of the men were not. He danced with wives in their fifties and sixties and their husbands thanked him for saving their evening.

He didn't meet the host until he'd been on board nearly an hour.

"Kender, this is too delightful," cried his current dance partner. "To think you've invited Ben Franklin! How Bostonian!"

Mr. Senneth — whom Ben Franklin had seen only from a distance, while he sold T's and Mitch rescued Miss Amnesia — smiled pleasantly enough at Ben. "I like a varied guest list," he agreed. "Ben, let me introduce you to a couple of other friends." He took Ben's arm, led him away from the gray-haired crowd, down the curving stairs and into the wheel room, where he said to Billy, "I think this gentleman has crashed our little party."

Hope awoke.

She awoke with a jolt like lightning bolts, and was catapulted right out of the bed.

The room was very dark.

The entire suite was very dark.

She ran down the hall, looked in the other bedroom, looked in the huge sitting area, the dining room, the . . .

Below and beyond the huge plate glass windows was Boston Harbor, and Long Wharf.

Lady Hope, lit and bedecked like a princess, was full of guests.

She could even see the dancers leaning on each other's arms. She could see the band and the glint of lanterns off the silvery rims of drums. She could see the whites of the crew and actually catch the twinkle of glasses, lined like troops on the uppermost deck bar.

And she could see Mitch, striding down the wooden docks, saluting the crew; yes, see him boarding *Lady Hope.*

He's crashing the party, she thought. To

see me. To dance with me and hold me and kiss me and get to know me better.

Hope knew the sensible thing to do. She knew the rational intelligent thing to do.

But more than she was a girl in danger, she was a girl in love.

I want Mitch to see me dressed up! I want him to see me in something beautiful, not that old pair of shorts. I want to dance with him and go for a midnight sail with him.

Look how civilized they are on that boat! Only good things happen to people who dance on yachts. So many witnesses. What could possibly go wrong among all those rich people?

Billy was courteous to Ben Franklin. He said softly, "Nobody wants any trouble. I understand how you'd enjoy this event. I enjoy a yacht, too. But you really do have to have an invitation to attend these parties, my friend. Now you're not going to be in any trouble, and we won't be calling the police. You and I will just walk casually down the steps, without disturbing any guests, and you don't come back." Billy smiled. "Got it?" He was friendly as a puppy. He reminded Ben of Derry.

Ben said, equally courteously, "I know you have Susan Nevilleson aboard, and the minute

I leave this boat, I'm going to be the one who calls the cops."

Billy's smile wavered, and then collapsed.

"I'm so sorry," he said immediately. The perfect yacht steward. "Please forgive me. I had no idea that Susan invited you. Of course, any friend of Miss Nevilleson is a friend of ours. I'll take you to her stateroom. She's still dressing for the party."

They went down a different circular stair, down below decks and, too late, Ben remembered how Derry had described the layout of the boat.

Susan felt the boat shift.

The engines began.

Her head was right up against pipes or exhausts. She could hear and feel every throb. She was forced to vibrate with every engine exchange. Michael had been correct. These were major engines.

We're going out to sea, thought Susan. Why not? Burial at sea is invisible and easy. You just weight the body. Down it goes.

But it's my body.

I don't want it going down.

Air began to seem wonderful to Susan. She could taste each breath she took, and she took deeper and deeper breaths, but not enjoying them, because the metallic taste of fear ruined each lungful.

She fixed her hair. She flung open the closet doors, and pulled out the indigo silk. She found no shoes that fit, so she wore her sandals. She would kick them off in the shoe basket before boarding. She took the elevator down. She hardly noticed the elegant marble, magnificent flowers, and uniformed doormen, not even the one who swung open the back doors for her. She saw only the image of herself and Mitch, the next act in her play, the final falling in love.

She ran lightly over the plaza, ducking between Jaguars and Mercedes parked there for the party, ran right down the dock and right up the steps. Crew she did not recognize — catering people, perhaps — stepped out of her way. And Billy, whom she recognized perfectly, simply gasped and did absolutely nothing. What could he do? A boat full of guests, the most important guests the Senneths would ever entertain? There could be no scenes at this party.

She would find Mitch in the crowd, she would waltz right off the boat with him, and together they would run to safety and to happily-ever-after.

She had just threaded through the guests, just climbed the circular stair to the dance floor, when something she had never thought of occurred.

Lady Hope left shore.

Chapter 11

Mitchell McKenna had never seen anything so beautiful. Hope was beyond mortal. She was a goddess, draped in silk, bronze hair heavy on her shoulders.

Mitch wanted a conversation with his father: Yes, Dad! There is love at first sight! I really love her, Dad. I have no idea what's going on with this girl, and what's more, I don't care.

Night had fallen. The sky had the pinkish glow of city lights — never really dark. And yet there were shadows everywhere, black and solid, and Hope was in relief against them: a sculpture carved against the water and the night.

He knew there was music; he could hear percussion, guitar, and singer. But mostly he heard only one syllable — Hope.

The yacht was jammed. Dancing was close and slow because there was no room for wild and fast. Okay with Mitch — they had a lifetime for wild and fast. He put his arms around her with such pleasure he thought that his whole life had been just a preparation for this. He said nothing, nor did she; they leaned against each other, and warmed each other.

The dance went on and on, their feet barely shifting, her head on his chest, his chin in her hair.

Mitch was so in love that he was in love with love, more than Hope. He was on a primitive physical level: feeling, touching, tasting, seeing — but not thinking. He didn't see Mr. Senneth. He didn't see Kaytha. He didn't see Ben Franklin. He didn't even feel *Lady Hope* leave the dock and gently turn and move among the shadows of the sea.

Hope saw even less. She knew only his cheek, his throat, and the silk of his jacket lapel. His hands gripped first her shoulders, and then her waist, and then shifted, restlessly, wanting everything.

My own T-Shirt God, she thought.

But Mitch was not wearing a T. He was wearing a black jacket with black silk lapels. If he had been handsome in a T-shirt, he was stunning in evening wear. She drew her hands down the lapels, down the silk, and he caught her hands in his.

"Hope, I can't wait till the symphony concert. I don't sell T's on Sunday. How about if you and I take a drive out to the country tomorrow? I'll pick you up at ten, okay? Wear jeans. We'll be very historic. It's the only thing you can be in Massachusetts."

He was rewarded by Hope's sweet smile.

Loveswept, each was sure that twenty-four hours of adoration was enough to expect a lifetime together.

Some party guests watched them with pleasure, remembering their own first love, happy for these beautiful strangers. Some were simply irritated, because the selfishness of love allowed them to take more than their share of space, and ignore everything around them.

As for the host and hostess, they were dumbfounded.

"What is happening?" said Kaytha. She was outraged. How dare they fall in love on her yacht? Hissing under her breath, she demanded, "*Who are they really?*"

Her father shook his head. "I haven't a clue."

Their fears had mounted like winds in a storm. Nothing in their previous museum arrangements had ever come to this. Their preparations — so careful, so detailed — prevented surprises. The world of fine art museums, and therefore the world of fine art thefts, moved very slowly.

Kender Senneth was coming unglued.

Kaytha could feel her father's layers separating, his resolve dissolving.

"Don't you come apart!" — She continued to call him Uncle Ken. It was a part of the game that appealed to Kaytha; made it far easier to deal with him — "Uncle Ken, you have a necklace to get back!"

He was hanging onto the rail, as if white knuckles could give him the strength to go on.

Hope was so beautiful! Remarkable. How astute of Kaytha to see that this was the daughter he should have had. This was how his little girl should have turned out! A perfect sculpture, artwork, a sweet good girl, who attracted sweet good boys, who was too innocent to know what her father did, and who would never have believed it if she were told.

"We'll let her watch while our unwanted bunkmates drown," said Kaytha. "That should bother her a little."

His own child, carrying his own genes, was a person who could kill.

He was still so chilled by the thought that he had to run from the thought. He said quickly, "But she doesn't know where the necklace is, Kaytha. That's the problem. She really has lost her memory."

"How do you know? How do you know it isn't a crock and a trick?"

"Because why, when she woke up in spite of the pills, didn't she go to the police? Kaytha, there is no logical intelligent reason for her to be here again. She must actually believe she is Hope Senneth."

Kaytha stared at the dancing partners. He was correct. There was no logical intelligent reason to come back. But when was love ever logical or intelligent?

In Kaytha, all three were now absent: love, logic, and intelligence were gone.

Which was when the message arrived from Billy. The caterer's lower-deck bartender came up to his employer. "Miss Senneth? Billy says he just acquired another guest for the bunkroom. Would you please come give him a hand with the sleeping arrangements?"

Kaytha had absolutely no idea who that other individual might be, but she knew one thing: She would give these particular guests a permanent sleep.

Oh, Ben! He was so handsome! She loved him in a tuxedo!

Of course, at that point, Susan would have loved him in a zebra costume.

If only she could call out, tell him how wonderful he was, tell him she adored him! Beneath the cruel strapping tape, she was laughing and giddy. *Oh, Ben! I'm so glad to see you!*

Billy held the gun very loosely, like a kid on Halloween. As if it were a toy.

It wasn't a toy.

They were the toys.

Oh, Ben, you can't rescue me. You're going to be caught up in this with me, instead. She loved him for it: for going so solidly into deep trouble. For her sake.

She didn't even glance at Billy, nor at the weapon he held, and when Kaytha took Billy's place, Susan didn't bother looking at Kaytha either. Ben Franklin was so much to look at. He was her answer to everything — and yet, he was as completely trapped as she, and the answer to nothing.

Oh, Ben, Ben! You shouldn't have liked me so much! You shouldn't have followed me, like a knight in shining armor rushing romantically into the dragon's cave!

But she was so glad that he had done it.

Proof that she was really loved. Loved beyond mere dates. Loved beyond rings or photos in a locket. She drank in the sight of Ben coming for her, Ben dressing and planning and crashing a party to carry her home — she wept with joy and fear for them both.

"Feast your eyes," said Kaytha. "Because you won't have him to see for long." Kaytha smiled. She held a long thin blade and, holding it, such a long, thin hand. Kaytha's hand.

"I am very accomplished with this knife," whispered Kaytha. Her smile perfectly matched the blade. Kaytha did not blink.

"You're in big trouble, big boy," she told Ben. "I'm not really angry with you, of course. You are nothing. Now you are out of time and will never be anything. But in the meantime, you are mine, and I am going to enjoy myself."

Kaytha was completely off the wall. Her sanity, if she had ever possessed it, was gone. The look in her eyes was so eager and yet so flat: as if she were a drawing of a person, but had no soul.

We are doomed, thought Susan. Mitch did this to us, with his romancing and his partying and his role-playing.

"Hello, sir," said Mitch, with the vague friendliness of lovers. He should have a courteous relationship with his girlfriend's father.

Mr. Senneth drew them away from the

dance floor and over near the bank of canvas-draped yacht toys. A row of lanterns changed the entire night for Mitch. Now Hope was no shadowy museum piece, but a vivid blue, her gown as deep and perfect as the blue of her yacht.

Hope's eyes moved toward Kender Senneth, wanting her father's approval also. Weird relationship, thought Mitch.

If anything, Kender Senneth was equally impressed. He stared at Hope as if seeing a ghost. After a long while, in a scratchy voice, like a record from the attic, he said, "The gown is beautiful, Hope. But it needs that missing necklace."

Mitch hugged Hope. "Well, when you find the necklace, Hope," he said happily, because everything made him happy right now, "let's go out and celebrate."

"How will we find the necklace?" asked Mr. Senneth. "I'd be most happy to enlist your assistance, Mitch."

"It must be some necklace," said Mitch. It would have to be, to match Hope's beauty. He suddenly remembered that he was crashing the party, and he flushed with embarrassment. "Mr. Senneth, I want to apologize for just coming on board. I know you didn't invite me. I know it's pretty rude. I . . . just . . . um — "

"Fell in love," said Mr. Senneth. "I remember feeling that way once. Toward Hope's mother." His eyes filled with tears. He walked away from them, the pressure of other people's love too much for him.

"Your poor dad," said Mitch sympathetically.

Hope came back to earth. Time to level with Mitch. She did not know how he would react when he found out he was in love with a fake. Would he feel tricked and laughed at? Would he despise her?

Not knowing the answer to that made her admit that she did not actually know Mitch McKenna at all. Her love frayed a little around the edges, was less secure, less wonderful.

"He's not my father," she whispered.

He sat on the nearest toy. The hull of a Wave Runner, he thought, pulling her down into his lap. He could hardly even look at Hope from so close. She was so beautiful he could not believe he had her.

Unexpectedly, he didn't hear Ginger's voice in his mind, but Susan's, answering Ben Franklin's question. Why would you kidnap a person you don't know? Either because *you do* know who she is, and she's rich and is worth a fabulous ransom, or because *it doesn't matter* who she is. You have evil plans for her no matter what.

Not her father.

Then what was going on?

It never crossed Mitch's mind to be afraid. He was excited. Delighted. Mystery and action and great lines. Yes!

"You see, I *did* hit my head," Hope was murmuring in his ear. "On the curb of the traffic island when I was watching that drive-by shooting thing. I fell down in traffic but somehow nobody ran over me and I managed to get back across the street. I ran through Quincy Market and finally sat down with something cold to drink and tried to stop trembling. I could have been killed! Or maimed or paralyzed! That was pretty exciting, so I spent a moment pretending I had been hurt horribly. Concussions. Cute doctors falling in love with me. Some long-term but not painful or disfiguring illness."

Mitch was laughing as silently as he could. "You drama major, you!"

"Truly. It's what I want more than anything. To act."

"Me, too," confided Mitch.

They were awestruck by this common ground, this proof of true love.

"So then what?"

"So then I decided on amnesia. And you walked up. And then this man appeared and claimed I was his daughter."

"Wait," said Mitch, starting to put this together, and finding a very long list of things he would never tell Ginger or his parents about Hope. "I thought you meant he was like your stepfather or your father's business partner or something. But you mean, you really aren't a Senneth? *You knew* you didn't know this man?"

Hope nodded.

"You knew that he knew you weren't his daughter? You knew that he had to know you were acting?"

"No, all he had to know was that I had amnesia. It was so exciting. Like being a counterspy, Mitch! And in The Jayquith!"

"You're crazy," breathed Mitch.

"Do you hate me?" she said anxiously.

"Where do you get that from? I adore you."

Slow dancing was a wonderful way to exchange information. It looked like kissing, or nibbling ears or laughing into each other's hair, and it was all of those things, but it was also listening to Hope. If he had not been intoxicated by her, if he had not been as interested in her kisses as her words, he might have done things differently.

But he didn't.

Derry had told Ben that these people were not accustomed to violence, and it was true.

For Billy left. The man with the strength and the gun *had walked away.*

How amazing, thought Ben, acting instantly, acting swiftly; for once in life, however, NOT acting.

Kaytha was completely unprepared to be kicked. He grabbed the wrist whose fingers held the knife, and then he slammed her against the unyielding mahogany door. In an instant, he'd taken her knife away. She was so frail and thin it was easy to hold both her wrists in one hand. With his free hand Ben Franklin grabbed the strapping tape lying visible on Susan's bunk. Using his teeth, he ripped off a strip and immobilized her wrists. He had tape over Kaytha's mouth within seconds. It took him only another moment to locate the handcuff key in her pocket.

A woman who never eats breakfast, lunch, or dinner cannot really stand up against a man who never misses them.

It was so quick there was no time for Kaytha to react, never mind call for reinforcements.

Ben was amazed. It must be true that criminals were stupid. It was incredibly stupid of these people to assume that they were in control and nobody could change that. He had changed it with the tip of his highly polished black shoes.

He unlocked Susan's handcuffs, and Susan, stunned, but not too stunned to react, unlocked Edie's. Then she set to work freeing her mouth.

"Now we leave the boat," said Ben. He didn't bother with the handcuffs for Kaytha. He used the rest of the roll of strapping tape and fastened her knees together, her ankles, her elbows. Susan thought how much it was going to hurt when that tape got ripped off and then she remembered that Kaytha was not a person to feel sorrow for.

"It's too late," said Edie. "We're out at sea. You can't run down the dock and call the police."

"We can't actually be out at sea," said Ben. "The harbor is huge. We've left the wharf, but we've got to be within reach of it. Come on, girls. Before Billy gets back."

Susan was massaging her wrists. Edie was not moving.

"Come on!" said Ben urgently.

"I'm staying," said Edie.

They stared at her.

"This is my family."

"Your insane murderous family," pointed out Susan. Her mouth hurt. Her body was trembling. Her knees were weak. She was cramped from the curved position of the bunk and from being fastened down — and probably from fear. She wasn't sure she could actually walk out of there.

Ben was not interested in Senneth family problems. He lifted Susan like a grocery bag, carrying her out the door with him, and up the tiny, curling stairs.

The stairs emerged at the far end of the main salon, right next to the wheelroom.

Billy was in the wheelroom.

Susan was still, ridiculously, in her colonial waitress costume. Hideously wrinkled and dirty, it fell now to cover her legs again and in the dark, if you hardly looked, she was just another woman in a long gown. Not, however, to Billy.

Ben went straight out the salon doors. They emerged on a narrow strip of deck, its varnish gleaming in the party lights, and there was nothing there. Nothing at all but water.

No land, no other boats, *nothing.*

The dark honey of the decks gleamed around them.

The guests were shadows, fluttering from

salon to library, fax room to lower deck, upper deck to aft bar.

And *Lady Hope*'s location was, as Edie had said, out to sea.

Ben and Susan did not even need to discuss it.

They stepped up to the railing as Billy stepped up to them, and vaulted into the churning cold green water of the Atlantic Ocean.

Chapter 12

The guests had had a lot of wine.

They had had a lot of everything else, too.

Although some were up on the high deck, stunned by the views and the skies and the stars, most had returned to the salons, where they were in hot pursuit of each other and each other's money.

Some guests were busy in the little library, where one was sending a fax and another was on the phone and a third was studying the marine maps. Two guests were in the deck house. There was a real wheel there, of the wonderful old-fashioned wooden type that are sometimes made into coffee tables. But there were also loran, radar, depth, speed and wind indicators, and enough other dials to resemble a jet cockpit. Rolled signal flags lay brightly in little slots, like bottles of wine.

The guests were mesmerized.

One woman said nervously to the steward that she thought somebody had gone overboard.

He smiled in a kindly fashion. "It can get noisy out here, can't it? And sounds over the water are certainly deceptive, aren't they?"

She felt like a fool.

"Are you a swimmer?" Ben Franklin asked.

Susan said, "Y."

"*Why*? Because we're in very deep water, very far from shore, that's why."

Susan giggled and blew out water like a whale. "YMCA," she said, "had the only pool in my town. I can swim in a nice clean chlorine-scented pool."

The Atlantic Ocean near Boston, Massachusetts, was not nice, not clean, and definitely not chlorine scented.

"Don't you feel as if something hideous is about to bite your toes?" said Susan, treading water.

"Yes, but unless it's a shark, I'd rather face it than Kaytha."

"Sharks?" whispered Susan.

"I'm sure they hate New England," said Ben Franklin.

They continued treading water. Susan said, "I'm not too fond of New England myself right now. Because that's fog coming in and surrounding us. Real thick serious fog. And I can't tell which way the shore is."

"The current will carry us."

"Yes, and what if the current is heading out to sea?" Susan pointed out.

"That's the trouble with you Harvard types. Always thinking of alternatives."

They took turns treading water, holding each other up. There seemed no point in using energy swimming when they might be swimming away from, rather than toward, safety.

"A hot July Sunday," said Ben Franklin. "And if we're out here long enough, you and I might actually freeze to death."

We're going to drown, thought Susan.

She could not think about it, about how her lungs would grab for air and find filthy salt water instead, about how it would feel, the pain and the terror, and how she would be sinking toward the unknown hideous bottom instead of being lifted into somebody's wonderful boat.

But she couldn't *not* think about it, either, and every thought she had was about her lungs or her flesh.

"Ben, I'm sorry I've never been nice."

"Me, too."

"Thank you for trying to save me."

"You're welcome."

"Ben, promise me something?"

"I don't think I'm in a position to promise anybody anything."

"Don't let go. When we sink, I don't want to sink all by myself."

"What are you doing?" said Mr. Senneth nervously.

"Going back," said the captain.

"Already?"

The captain shrugged his eyebrows. "I don't think those two will get picked up, not at this hour, not with the fog coming, not with the tide going out. But I also think it's time we docked, waved good-bye to our guests, packed our bags, and blew this town."

"What about the necklace?" demanded Mr. Senneth.

The captain looked at him incredulously. "You lost the game, Ken. Lost by a big margin. We maybe could have kept going if Kaytha hadn't started taking prisoners, but come on! It's over. We have to bail out fast."

"I can't give up this name," protested Kender Senneth. "I've built it up for nine years! I've got contacts in six countries under this name."

"No contacts who will write to you if you

go to prison," the captain pointed out. "You stay in town if you want, Ken, but I'm taking out my other passport and then I'm taking a taxi to the airport. You will, too, if you think about it."

"I want the necklace!" he said.

"You never had the necklace. You had your fake."

"The exchange is Tuesday," he said. "I know we can hang on till then. I can make the girl tell me where it is."

The captain looked at him and knew how he would make the girl tell where the necklace was. He said, "Don't start till I'm gone, Ken."

"I have approximately six million more questions, but first I think we — "

"Excuse me," said one of the musicians.

"Oh, are we in your way?" said Mitch.

"No, no, I just wondered if you could help me haul this down the stairs." She was small for carrying rock-band equipment. The amplifiers were as heavy as she was.

"Oh, sure," said Mitch, seeing no problem. Expecting to be right back. Acting as if he were still a nineteen-year-old living a normal teenage boy's life. Acting, against all evidence, as if people on the *Lady Hope* were what they seemed.

* * *

The sounds were fat. Puffy overweight sounds: bloated horns and soggy wind.

The view continued to be what it had been: nothing. Visibility zero. So that's what it meant.

"Ben, I feel as if I've spent my whole life with zero visibility," said Susan. "Now when I could see things more clearly, and care about the right things, and I know what counts and what doesn't . . . now I'm really at zero visibility. Forever."

"It would count to me if we sank using real names," Ben said.

"Rusty Corder can't be your real name. Rusty's a nickname, too, isn't it?"

"Short for Walter."

"Walter," she repeated. She began giggling. "You really stepped out of line when they were giving out the good names, didn't you?"

He shrugged. It made him bob down in the water. "I was named for someone good," he said.

Susan thought that was the most beautiful sentence she had ever heard. Named for someone good. Will anybody name a daughter for me? she thought, and years later that little girl will say, *I was named for someone good?*

I'm out of time, she thought. I wanted to

do good in the world, be worthy of having a girl named for me, and all I am going to do is sink.

The top of Mitch's head was still visible, going down the tiny stairs, when the captain came smiling to Hope's side. "And did the most beautiful lady on board enjoy my boat?" he said.

She beamed at him.

"It's traditional for the captain to ask a few guests to stay on after the party to salute the boat," he said. "I'll ask Mitch to join us, of course. Let's retire to the Arabian Room."

An Arabian Room! Really, the yacht held untold surprises, one after another!

The captain clapped a hand over her mouth before she could see it coming, grabbed her arms, and forced her down an opening in the deck. It was a glass-lidded hatch she had not even noticed. In the space below, Billy caught her legs, yanked her through, and swept her into a stateroom she'd never seen.

Each guest was personally escorted off the yacht.

"*Lady Hope* is such a beautiful boat," said the guests. "Thank you so much for having us, Kender."

"Lovely time," they cried, waving, "wonderful company!"

"What happened to that darling little Ben Franklin?"

"He went home early," said Mr. Senneth. "You know how the elderly like their sleep."

Everybody chuckled, and waved, and thanked once more.

The caterers packed up. Billy and Kaytha began a sweep of the boat, to make sure nobody was hidden on board. Kaytha's face had a horrible red strip, two inches wide, where the skin had torn when Billy peeled back the tape. Her wrists and elbows were painfully raw. But she was smiling. "We have Hope," she explained.

"You've done enough damage, Kaytha. I'll deal with her."

"No," said Kaytha Senneth. "You're kind. You don't know how to do this. You want to find some nice soft easy way out. Well, she knows where that necklace is! And there's no soft easy way out. I'll handle it."

Kaytha said, "Where is Mitch, Hopester?"

"He went home," said Hope. She was hideously afraid. Where *was* Mitch? The Senneths were onto her, and he was not here.

"I find it hard to believe he could tear himself

away from you," said Kaytha. "Ten minutes ago, you two were super-glued together. Where is he now?"

Hope pasted on a happy smile, busily being the silly pathetic teenager in love. "He's gone on home to get a good night's sleep. He'll come for me in the morning. We're going to drive out to Concord and see where Ralph Waldo Emerson and Henry David Thoreau and Louisa May Alcott lived."

"No, Hopey," said Kaytha, smiling right back. "You're not."

She was stating a fact. She knew. Hope wanted to scream. Instead she kept up her act. "He promised, Kaytha," she protested, wide-eyed and eager.

"*We* didn't. Do you really think you're going to have this life? Do you really think you're going to go on being Hope Senneth, and having parties, and going on dates? Of course not. Your little allotment of time is up now, Hopesy."

The master stateroom was immense. A California king bed was squarely in the middle, surrounded by glistening silver shelving. A tiny vertical bar opened up inside a circular silver pillar. A television set was neatly fixed in the paneled ceiling, so you could lie in bed, your pillow resting on a special angled headboard, and watch movies in perfect comfort. Down the silvered bookshelf ran a row of a hundred movie tapes, and inside the angled headrest were CDs, video games, and paperback novels. The bed itself was covered in cloth of black and silver. It was sort of Arabian, like a sheik's tent.

"You may scream if you like," said Mr. Senneth. "Nobody can hear you. There are no windows or openings on this level. Any sound you make will be muffled by the construction of the boat, and by the fact that we are actually below the water line."

"It's time to tell us where the necklace is, Hope," said Kaytha. Her stare was so frightening that, to get away from it, Hope sat down on the edge of the bed. Kaytha immediately sat also, as if they were little cars stuck on the same track.

"We're bringing Dr. Patel on board," said Mr. Senneth. "A few injections and you should be chatting away about the necklace. It would spare you considerable pain if you simply talked about it now."

Hope had a feeling that Dr. Patel usually saw Kaytha. Often. Would the doctor be willing to listen to her? She must know that Hope Senneth didn't exist.

Oh, that would be a fine sentence to use on

a psychiatrist, she thought. Hi, I don't exist, but —

"Talk!" hissed Kaytha.

"I'm happy to talk," said Hope, "but I explained to you over and over that I don't remember who I am! You're the ones who claimed me. You're the ones who insist that I am Hope Senneth. You came out onto that plaza and said Yes, this is my daughter, come home to The Jayquith." She let herself cry again. "I'm so sorry that Edie stole your necklace. I'm so sorry that I don't still have it. But you're talking about things I don't remember!"

For a moment they still believed her. It was sweet praise, in a way, that she could still, with all that had happened, maintain her act.

"Fine," said Kaytha. "But I'm not angry now over the necklace, or even over Hope Senneth, who doesn't exist. But because you took Mitch from me."

The knife seemed as huge as an executioner's blade. The only thing more scary than the knife was the look in Kaytha's eyes.

"So now, my dear cuz, I assure you I'm eager to use this knife between your little ribs."

Hope dissolved. "All right! All right, I'll tell you! I never had amnesia. I made it all up. I'm fine, I always was. Just don't use that knife. Mr. Senneth, don't let her use that knife, please — "

"It was a scam?" he said. "The whole thing was a con?"

She was astonished to see that he was pleased. Proud, even, as if she were his daughter, and had proved herself worthy.

"I've spent my life conning people," said Mr. Senneth. "I'm very good. It's a pity, Hope, that there is no Hope, and that you and I will never work together again. You are an artist." He meant this. He was comparing himself, a con artist, to painters and sculptors.

"The amnesia was a crock?" said Kaytha. "You tricked us?"

Time. She had to gain time. Surely Mitch had plans, surely he was calling the police or the cavalry or the coast guard or whoever you called in Boston, Massachusetts.

"Kaytha," she said, "if I'm not Hope Senneth, who is? Who was she? Whose passport is it?"

"My mother's," said Kaytha. "My mother had a hard time facing life. She decided not to go on living last year."

"And you watched?" said Hope, remembering the hatred Kender Senneth felt.

Kaytha slashed down hard with the knife, but Hope grabbed a bed pillow and she held it between her and the blade like a shield.

The knife sliced into the pillow, a great crescent of silver going down, and a spill of feathers wafted into the room. Kaytha laughed. "Make a wish," she teased Hope. "Catch one, like a falling star or a milkweed seed. Make a wish. I will decide what comes true, of course. So chances are, your wishes won't come true. But you could try."

She was insane. You could see it. Hope had not known that insanity could be visible.

"You didn't really need to act, did you?" Hope said to Mr. Senneth. "After what Kaytha has put you through, accepting a daughter with amnesia was nothing."

"I was the actress!" said Kaytha. "You were nothing! I saw you down there, I saw what happened, and when Billy phoned us from the yacht phone to say that you didn't know who you were, I said, Fine, then, *we'll* know who she is! We'll know for her! I plotted the whole father/daughter/cousin thing in two minutes! It was my script!"

"You were brilliant," said Hope.

"Yes, I was," said Kaytha. "But my father likes having you for a daughter more than he likes having me."

Hope thought this was reasonable of him.

"So I'm getting rid of you. It won't hurt if you tell me where the necklace is first."

She did not dare tell them where the necklace was.

It had shaken Mitch terribly to get back up to the deck and find no Hope. No Mr. Senneth. No Kaytha. They hadn't left *Lady Hope,* he was sure of that. He had to get help, but he couldn't leave the yacht to do it; he had to be sure Hope was okay, take her with him. He was strong. He could shove any of these people overboard, if need be.

Except that one of them had a gun.

Mitch ducked into the engine room.

He knew it well, having spent many hours here when his parents owned *Starry Night.* Parts of the engine had been rebuilt, and he approved. His plan was to wait until the place was quiet, and then summon the coast guard on the modem in the wheel room. He'd say it was drugs, even though he knew now it was the necklace, whatever the necklace meant, or was. The coast guard would be here in a second. They were only a few wharves away. Maybe just to be sure he'd also fax something to the customs office at Fosters Wharf.

He'd have the boat overrun in a minute.

Scrunched in his corner, he planned and considered.

He did not plan to feel a cold small circle pressed against the nape of his neck.

Billy's revolver.

Chapter 13

"Susan?" repeated Mitch. *"Susan Nevilleson?"* They had forced him to lie on the floor face down, the way they did in cop shows, when they've caught the guy running through the woods. There was no tape left to bind him, and the little plastic handcuffs were too small to go around wrists the size of Mitch's.

Billy's gun, however, was not too small to keep Mitch lying down.

Mitch could not believe he had endangered Susan like that. Please God, don't let it be true! he thought. I just used her name to impress Mr. Senneth. Please don't let Susan be dead. Please don't let me be the reason Susan died.

"Susan," he whispered.

The white carpet in the master stateroom was so nubbly, he could feel the separate bumps of it against his cheek.

Susan, who had wanted success as much as anybody he'd ever met, who had a map of her life, all the roads and rivers of hope. Susan, who had dreamed of true love and lockets. Susan, who had wanted her own stage, her own theater, her own television show. Susan, so exhausted by her job, but never pitying herself, always charging on, always fun . . . Susan.

Everything Mitch had chosen not to think about in his friendship with Susan pressed into his mind the way the carpet pressed into his cheek. Susan had loved him.

And how had he repaid her?

By using her — even less than that! By using her name — in such a way that she died from it.

Susan, he thought, as if repeating her name would somehow turn the tide and bring her home safely.

Hope was in the room with him; they were all there — Hope, Kaytha, Mr. Senneth, Edie, and Billy — but he could not think of Hope. For her — for her beauty, which had overpowered him; for her mystery, which had so appealed to him — for her he had done this ridiculous small thing which had had such a terrible ending.

Why? he thought. Was I really trying to

rescue a girl in trouble, a damsel in distress? Or was I just trying to prove I could act? Just using the stage set of The Jayquith, and the lines that Hope handed me?

Using.

I did nothing for Susan at all, in the end, except to use her.

Oh, Susan!

Kaytha watched his face with interest. She couldn't identify with emotions. Kaytha had never felt guilt or grief. Kaytha felt other people existed in order for her to use them, and and could not have followed Mitch's reasoning: that using Susan had led to her demise.

So what?

It happens.

Meanwhile, Mitch had a good run for his money.

Kaytha debated the best way to get Hope to tell them where the necklace was. Of course, if Hope really didn't remember, it was a moot point.

Hope was so proud of her looks. So Kaytha would begin by removing those good looks. She would start easy, with the hair. That gorgeous incredible bronze-brown hair. Kaytha would cut it all off. Then she would shave a matching asp, curling around and around

Hope's naked skull. Hair grows back, Hope would tell herself, I'll be okay, it's just hair . . . but Hope would be wrong.

Kaytha was also tempted by Mitch.

How wonderful that this T-shirt god, this big, muscular blond piece of perfection, had ended up helpless on the floor.

Kaytha walked around Mitch's prone body and knelt on the carpet. The nubbly white wool joined them, as if they were swimming in the same pool. How funny he looked, flattened out. Now he could see two things: Billy's gun and Kaytha's knife.

Kaytha smiled.

Hope was sitting cross-legged on the immense bed. Its headboard was slanted padded mahogany, so that readers or television watchers need not even stack pillows to be in the perfect position, but merely recline. Mr. Senneth had simply used two bathrobe sashes to fasten Hope to the headboard. She could not believe that it had been so easy for him, nor that it was so impossible for her to free herself.

She preferred thinking about physical things: her wrists, whose strength from tennis no longer mattered; her back, which far from being at a comfy angle, was awkwardly, and by now very painfully, arched because of the tying up.

But if her time on earth was running out, she could not allow herself the luxury of pretending this was only a physical problem. She had to face what she had done.

For kicks — like a person joyriding, and accidentally taking an innocent bystander over the cliff with him — *for kicks* she had embarked on this. For no reason except to see what would happen. Not a single thought for what might happen to other people, helplessly drawn in. Just the desire to act it out.

She had always despised rotten little junior high boys who, in guidance counselor terms, "acted out." Oh, they have troubles at home, the counselors would say, alcoholic parents, so they're "acting out." What contempt she had for them, inflicting their personal problems on entire classes, just because they had no self-discipline to go on bravely like everybody else.

I'm worse than anybody, she thought. Acting out in junior high just meant ruining a class here and there. Acting out my spy drama, acting out my amnesia farce . . . a girl named Susan has died. I don't even know who Susan is! I don't even know how this happened, or what she went through. But whatever hopes and dreams Susan Nevilleson had are at the bottom of Boston Harbor.

She made herself look further at the consequences of her silliness. Silly was not the right word. She had gone way beyond silly, entertaining herself with her own stage play. Acting, she thought, has to stay on Broadway. You can't move it into people's lives without hurting them. Of course, I've learned the lesson a little late for all of us.

She thought of her parents, who had said New York isn't safe. You're to go to small town New England. Drama is ridiculous. You are to interview at colleges with a math major in mind. You can be an accountant or a tax attorney; they always find work. Forget acting.

So what had their sweet, good daughter done?

Their daughter who never disobeyed, never rebelled?

Picked another dangerous city; picked her own little drama; thought of nothing but acting; and then, acted out.

Her poor real-life parents' next act . . . what would that be? Choosing her coffin?

"Susan and her boyfriend were not murdered," said Mr. Senneth huffily, as if Kaytha were totally misrepresenting the situation. "Nobody here has ever done such a thing, and nobody here ever will. The girl and her boyfriend jumped overboard. They chose that. Nobody forced them. And the fog was rolling in. We could not possibly have found them. I'm afraid it really comes under the heading of suicide. I cannot be held responsible for this."

Instinctively, Mitch tried to roll over to look at the speaker, but Billy's gun immediately made skin contact with Mitch's nose.

They froze in position for a moment. Mitch surrendered and flattened himself again, while Kaytha giggled.

Mitch said, "Susan's boyfriend?"

His tone of voice was so confused that it confused the others. "The one who impersonates Benjamin Franklin," said Mr. Senneth. "You're all impersonating people, of course. I have no idea who you really are, young man. The Jayquith was not able to find records for me that a Mr. and Mrs. McKenna ever stayed there, let alone on the seventh floor!"

"*Ben was with her?*" cried Mitch.

"He's probably still with her," said Kaytha, still crouching, enjoying the way Mitch screwed up his eyes to keep the tears from coming. The way the tears came anyway, and sopped down into the rug. "At the bottom of the deep blue sea," she sang.

"You are sick," said Hope.

Edie floated from one side of the stateroom to the other. Edie was, like Kaytha, too thin. And she had a frizzy look to her: as if not just her hair, but also her thinking, had split ends.

Hope couldn't figure out why the other Senneths paid no attention to Edie. Edie had started the whole nightmare; and free like this, she could just dash off the boat and call the police and end the whole nightmare. Why didn't she? Edie had a part to play and she wasn't doing it.

She won't save us, thought Hope. She won't even know what's happening. Two days tied up in the bunk with Kaytha flicking her knife had finished her off. She isn't dead, but she is brain dead.

Edie had run out of energy and courage. And the Senneths knew it.

Kaytha tucked the knife blade back into its ivory sheath and then flicked it out again. She repeated this twice more. It was a good show.

"Hope, tell them!" said Mitch. "Tell them where the necklace is."

I'm going to have to act again, thought Hope. Acting got me into this. Acting will have to get us out. She said, "Mitch — believe me — I . . . "

"Believe you?" cried Mitch. "Give me a break. Who could believe you on anything now?" His muscles prepared again to turn, so he could face her. Billy, pressing the gun now into Mitch's cheek, prevented him from trying. Mitch was panting, as if in the midst of a wrestling match, and perhaps he was: a wrestling match with himself, a wrestling match to keep himself down, lest the gun go off.

When you grew up in the mountains, you grew up comfortable with guns: your father and uncles and brothers and neighbors hunted. So Hope knew that Billy was not comfortable with the gun he held. He was afraid of it.

But an enemy who can't handle guns is even worse than an enemy who can. Anything might happen. And that gun might be pointed at Mitch, or at Hope, or Billy's own foot, and Billy would hardly know.

Not only was Mr. Senneth not used to violence, even Billy was no expert. She wondered if Billy, too, was an artist. Not a con artist, but a copier of necklaces. Or was he the salesman? The one who found the buyers? Because he was neither sailor, nor thug.

"I thought you were nice people!" cried Hope to Mr. Senneth.

"We usually are. Edie put us in a difficult position and I admit that we have responded poorly. We didn't have time to think things through. We do not normally use violence. We just want to make a very large amount of money. You, however, have obstructed us."

"And we're running out of time here," said Billy. The hand holding the weapon trembled. "Where is the necklace, Hope?"

It was interesting that they continued to call her Hope, and that she continued her own act, considering herself to be Hope. They were half on stage, and half off. It was like Ben Franklin, who had remained Ben Franklin to his friends after he shed the costume. He would never shed his nickname now.

She said, "I don't understand why you people don't just quit. Surely so much has gone wrong now that you — "

"Who are you to second guess us?" shrieked Kaytha, suddenly vaulting up from the floor and landing with a bounce on the bed. She stayed tucked, like a gymnast. The bed lurched when she hit the mattress and Hope knew why they had made her sit cross-legged; it would take such time to unfold herself.

Kaytha said, "How much do you like her, Mitch?"

There was a point beyond which acting could not go. He was being handed lines, but this was beyond improv, and Mitch McKenna did not know what to say.

"All right," said Hope. "I'll explain everything."

Billy tilted back a little, as if he needed space in which to listen. Mr. Senneth half-sat on one of the ledges that held VCR tapes and books. Kaytha turned her face somewhat, to hear better with one ear aimed directly at the speaker. Edie curled up in the single armchair, like a child ready for a bedtime story.

Hope began at the beginning. "I was born in Appalachia. My family is . . ."

Nobody told her to cut to the chase. Nobody said: Hey, we don't care, huh? You don't even need to tell us your name, because you're going to be buried at sea and we don't need a name for that. For if they told her it didn't matter — she and Mitch were doomed whatever she said — why tell them? They had to let her talk, in order to get to the talk they needed.

She told them about poverty. About yearning for riches. About dreaming of a wealthy man. About coming to the city to find the gold, so to speak.

And there it was. Gold. Handed to her. Placed right in her linen handbag, as if decreed by the gods. It was hers, gold and rubies and emeralds fit for a queen.

As Hope described the necklace, giving the ultimate detailed proof that Yes! she remembered, and Yes! she had respected their work, their faces softened. This necklace was everything to them. It was more than life and logic.

"I wanted the necklace," said Hope. "Of course I wanted the necklace. But more than that, I wanted the people who had necklaces like that. I wanted your life! I wanted suites at The Jayquith and yachts that cruised the world. I wanted gowns designed for that necklace and parties to wear the necklace to."

She said, "I wanted you."

They stared at each other: the real Senneths and the false one.

They were as spellbound as if they had never heard this story.

The silence curled around her like a tongue of silk.

Kaytha's disagreeable high voice said, "Yes, but where *is* it?"

"I went back to the train station," said Hope, "where my suitcase was stashed in a locker. I left my bag, with the necklace, in the locker. Then I went to the Boston Public Library, and walked through the stacks to a dark and dusty place where the books are dull and nobody wants them. I hid the locker key in the pocket of a book that hasn't gone out in years. As soon as the library opens, we can — "

"You what? You idiot!" cried Kaytha. "What if somebody does take that book out?"

"But tomorrow is Sunday," said Mr. Senneth. "The Library does not open. We have to wait until Monday."

"I'm sure they have Sunday hours," said Kaytha quickly. "I'll call them."

It was two in the morning.

The master stateroom, of course, had a telephone, and the Library's friendly recording announced the hours it was open.

"Two to six," said Kaytha, breathing the words like a safe combination. "Two to six," she repeated. She flicked her knife. "Now which book is the key in, Hopey?"

"I'll have to show you," she said. The telephone was right behind her tied arms. Tucked right inside the headboard with all the other electronic equipment, the amazing selection of adult toys that the *Lady Hope* featured. If she could get at the phone . . .

"Oh, of course. Silly me. Going to keep yourself alive, are you? Going to give yourself a few more hours, are you? Planning on screaming for help in the middle of a crowded public building, are you? Well, think again, Hopesy." Kaytha giggled again.

"What are you two idiots doing?" came the shout. A thick yellow glow, a muffled flash-light, zeroed in on them.

Ben Franklin had never been so glad to be called an idiot. They could call him anything, any time, as long as they pulled him out of the water.

He was too tired to answer, and Susan, shivering in his arms, could not even lift an arm to wave.

It was a genuine fishing boat, and it stank. Rotted and oily, slick with fish guts. Ben Franklin could have hugged the boat itself, along with the crew.

The crew shoved them into a very hot tiny cabin, wrapping them both in the same dirty blanket and pouring coffee out of a thermos.

They had been in the water for hours. Ben knew there were terribly important things to tell his rescuers, terribly important . . . something . . . he had to notify . . . or call . . . or something . . . but . . . but he slept.

In the same blanket, he and Susan fell into the same deep sleep: the comatose overwhelming sleep from exhaustion and fear.

But not the sleep of death.

Chapter 14

"I can't believe you're desecrating the *Lady Hope* like this!" screamed Hope. "This beautiful yacht, this lovely *Lady Hope.* You can't commit murder on her!"

"Just watch," said Kaytha.

Hope's fingers, back behind the slanted headboard, tried Braille. When you are accustomed to eyesight, you don't know things by feel. You have no memory in your fingertips. She struggled and struggled, but her fingertips told her nothing. Not one bump, not one raised spot. The clues were there, but she could not read them.

"Please, please, please," cried Hope, "I'll tell you anything, I promise. Don't kill Mitch. I'll go with you and we'll get into the train station locker and I'll give you the necklace."

Kaytha remained unimpressed. "Press that against his ear, Billy," said Kaytha.

Billy flinched.

"No!" whispered Hope.

"No," said Mr. Senneth, even more feebly.

Kaytha said, as if she were being extremely reasonable, "Tell me exactly what book."

Finally a book title entered Hope's head, along with the Dewey Decimal number. It was from her last history project. She could picture it in her bibliography, down toward the bottom of the page. "*The Robber Barons,*" she said, breathing heavily.

"It's 973.8," Hope added quickly. "It's about railroad magnates and people who founded industries and things. Nobody cares anymore, you don't have to worry that anybody touched it. It's black and very dusty and the corners of the book are crushed in."

Kaytha ran the knife very gently down Mitch's arm. Billy said, "Kaytha, don't, she's telling us." Billy pressed the barrel against Mitch's cheek.

"Kaytha!" Hope shrieked. "I just told you where the Queen Isabella necklace is. *Don't kill him.* Just because you killed Ben and Susan doesn't mean you have to go on killing! You can stop, Kaytha. Please please don't kill again."

"I don't believe what you said," said Kaytha.

"What do I have to do to prove I'm telling

the truth?" screamed Hope. "Don't kill him, Kaytha Senneth!" she shouted, as if to call the girl back to sanity with her full name.

Mr. Senneth said, "Hope. What is with this little rundown? Naming the yacht? Naming Kaytha, naming Susan and Ben, naming — " he leaned over her, yanked hard, and jerked back the tilted headboard.

The yacht, of course, offered every twentieth century amenity. Not just individual heat and air-conditioning controls, not just remotes for VCR and radio, but also the telephone.

Whose receiver lay separated from the phone.

Mr. Senneth hung it up. "Whom did you dial?" he said conversationally.

"Nine-one-one, of course," said Hope, glaring at him. "That's a regular phone line! And it dials regular shore numbers. And they've heard every bit of this."

"Kill them both," said Mr. Senneth to Kaytha. "Then we have to leave. The limousine is still in the hotel parking lot. I believe we have sufficient time."

"They'll track you," said Mitch from the floor. "They'll have your names. They'll have — "

"They'll have nothing," said Mr. Senneth.

"We have never used our real names. Get rid of him, Kaytha."

About all Ben could wake up enough to do was call his parents. "You live near here?" said Susan. "Did I know that?"

"No," said Ben, "I never talk about my family."

"Why not?" said Susan. "Are they embarrassing?"

"They're rich. Embarrassingly rich. We live on Louisburg Square. You're going to love it, Susan. You'll get me and millions, too."

"You're fibbing, aren't you?"

He grinned. "From here to San Francisco. We live in a third floor, shanty walk-up in the worst part of town. You want millions, you're going to have to go back to Mitch."

"Mitch, ugh. He got us into this. He — "

"Mitch!" said Ben Franklin. "That's what we have to do. Make sure Mitch and Miss Amnesia are okay."

He grabbed the phone again.

"I personally," said Susan, "think Mitch deserves whatever he gets. How happy were you out there in the water waiting to drown?"

Ben grinned. "Somebody has to be best man at my wedding."

* * *

Why had he been so passive? What on earth had made him lie there as if he himself were the well-trained collie?

Mitch spun around, flinging Kaytha against Billy's feet. Grabbing Billy's ankles, he gave a tremendous jerk. The gun went off, Hope screamed, Kaytha swore, and Billy fell. Hard.

Mitch couldn't see the gun. Where had it fallen?

Kaytha definitely knew where the knife was. She raised it.

He remembered thinking to himself, I could whip this girl with a restaurant toothpick. The knife was nothing but a very long toothpick. Leaping back out of her range, Mitch simply took the thick foam padding off the ledge, doubled it over, and used it for a shield. The knife pierced his foam rubber easily, but stayed there. Mitch disarmed her.

It took a few moments. He was aware that he was vulnerable to Billy, the gun, Mr. Senneth, and Edie. But nobody attacked him. Panting, as he held Kaytha, he looked around — and saw nobody.

"They left," said Hope.

Mitch cut the bathrobe sashes that held her down.

The little tan handcuffs that had been too small for Mitch were exactly right for Kaytha.

Hope and Mitch went up on deck.

No police arrived.

No rescue services appeared.

No sirens screamed.

"Did you really telephone 911?" said Mitch.

Hope nodded.

"What do you bet you got a wrong number?" They both laughed.

"This whole thing has been a wrong number," said Hope.

When the boat docked, a single small person came up the steps onto *Lady Hope*'s deck. It was Derry. "Derry, the deckhand," said Mitch tiredly. "You missed the action, kiddo."

"I'm not a kid. I work with a museum in Paris and I'm trying to locate the Renoir painting the Senneths stole last year."

Hope could hardly believe it. Was there anything the Senneths had not done? Any museum from which they had not pulled off thefts and substitutions? "One of us really was a spy?" marveled Hope. "Derry, you didn't add things up fast enough. The show is over and the cast left town. They took Edie. They were right about her a week ago — she was coming apart, she's just a liability. Kaytha's been left behind, but nobody will get anything out of her. I can't tell you where the Renoir is. Nobody mentioned paintings around me."

"Where are Ben Franklin and Susan?" said Derry anxiously.

The adrenaline rush that had allowed him to overpower Kaytha and Billy vanished. Mitch was overpowered again, but this time by grief. Oh, Ben! he thought, mourning his friend. Oh, Susan! And it's my fault, my fault!

Derry called the museum first, and the police second. Nobody arrived very speedily. Hope was not reassured. When you called the police, shouldn't they instantly round the corner on two wheels?

Ben and Susan got there first . . . by taxi.

Mitch bellowed with joy and relief, beating on his chest like Tarzan. He hugged Ben so hard he nearly crushed ribs.

"I hope you have money, Mitch," said Ben, removing himself from the hug, "because I don't have anything with me to pay the taxi fare. I didn't drown, but my wallet did."

Mitch hugged Susan, a little less hard.

"Taxi fare," he muttered, dragging it out. "If I had written a script," said Mitch, "there would have been much more drama than a taxi at the end."

"A huge fire," agreed Hop[illegible]
explosion. *Lady Hope* sinking like the [illegible]
her jewels lost forever and ever."

Mitch paid the driver and started to put his wallet back into his pants pocket, but Susan stopped him. "You'd better have lots and lots of money," said Susan, "because I'm suing you for sixty trillion dollars for emotional pain and suffering."

Mitch hugged her once more. "I'm sorry. Are you ever going to talk to me again?"

"Not in this lifetime, buddy."

"She holds a grudge," Ben Franklin explained.

"How about if I take everybody out to dinner? We'll get a pizza."

"Walter and I are not settling for pizza, Mitchell," said Susan.

You knew you were in trouble when they called you Mitchell. He said, "Who's Walter? I thought I knew the cast, but — "

"Me," said Ben Franklin. "I'm going by my real name now."

"Then who was Rusty Corder?" said Hope.

"More to the point," said Ben Franklin, "who was Hope?"

"Hope was Kaytha's mother and Mr. Senneth's wife. She died last year. There was a passport for Hope Senneth, and she looked thirty-five in it because she was thirty-five when the photo was taken. Mr. Senneth just kept his thumb over the birthdate and Mitch and I were too dumb to think of checking that. I was so dizzy I thought maybe I really *was* Hope."

"She is dizzy," Susan said to Mitch. "I don't know what Ginger is going to say about her."

Mitch thought of all the things Ginger would say, and grinned. The good part was going to be bringing Hope into his real life, getting off stage, throwing away roles. Being themselves.

"Oh, yeah," he said, finally getting around to a very important fact. "Hope — who are you?"

"I want you to keep calling me Hope," she said. "I love the name Hope."

"So do I," he said. "But I have to know who you really are. It matters."

"But I'm really boring."

Mitch shook his head. He gave her his world-class grin. "This weekend has been a lot of things, but boring isn't one. Unforgettable is closer. And when you come to school in Boston, you and I will have a totally non-boring love life. Promise." He kissed her hair and cheeks.

"I promise. But I still want to ...
She kissed his ears and throat.

"No. We're going to go to your college interviews, you're going to go to school here, so we can date, and I'm dating whoever you really are. That's that. Non-negotiable."

"I agree," said Susan. "The name Hope is ruined for me. Who are you really?"

She didn't want to come all the way off the stage. She had loved parts of Hope. The wealth, the classiness, the splendor of it. The fabulous hotel suite, the yacht named for —

Not named for me, she reminded herself. Nothing there was named for me. Hope Senneth is dead, and she was a desperate, sad woman with a dreadful family. Whereas I am alive, and very very lucky to be alive, and I'm a happy person with a wonderful family.

"Lynne Cook," she said at last. "Dull, boring, reliable old Lynne Cook."

Susan rolled her eyes. "Whatever else you are, Lynne Cook, you are not reliable, dull, or boring. Forget it. You are a ditzy nutty crazy piece of work." Susan laughed suddenly. "And a terrific actress."

Of course what interested the police and the museum most — once they realized they weren't going to find Kender Senneth on the yacht or in The Jayquith — was the necklace.

"It's in your train station locker?" said the chairman of the board of the museum. He was deeply humiliated because he had been the one to name Kender Senneth to the board. Judge of character had not turned out to be his strong suit.

"Well, no, actually, it's not," said Lynne Cook, blushing. "I thought it was junk. It's very very ugly. It's incredibly huge, and the stones aren't cut neatly like diamond engagement rings, and the gold is so thick and ropey I knew it had to be fake, and who on earth would ever wear a thing like that anyway? It was tacky and pathetic."

The museum director closed his eyes.

"I thought it was pretend. Halloween jewelry. For if you want to dress up like a princess. Stuff you'd buy at a tag sale from some person with really bad taste."

"And?" said the museum director.

"It was heavy," said Lynne.

"Meaning?" said the museum director.

"I stuck it in the Salvation Army bin. I thought maybe somebody would want to pay a quarter for it and I didn't want to keep carrying it."

They were helplessly laughing. Queen Isabella's necklace, for whom they all might have died, too tacky to carry around.

"Good thing you had the fake one," said the museum director.

"So the Senneths could never have done the switch anyway," said Mitch.

"No, but, Mitch, if Kaytha had realized that, if I had admitted it, she'd have dropped us overboard in a heartbeat."

Mitch doubted it. Dropping people overboard was too easy for Kaytha.

The police were not able to follow the reasoning that had led Lynne Cook into this adventure. "I guess because there was no reasoning," she said, unable to meet their eyes. "I didn't reason. I just acted."

"Your real parents must be worried sick," said one cop.

"No, because I promised to call Sunday night. Even though so much has happened, it's only Sunday dawn. They haven't even gotten around to worrying about me yet."

"You are truly an idiot," said the policeman. He stared at her with narrow eyes, memorizing her idiocy, so he could teach his own daughter not to act like that.

"I know," said Lynne Cook humbly.

"But you met me that way," said Mitch. "We wouldn't have met if you hadn't been an idiot. I like idiots."

The policeman said, "There is nothing more annoying than love at first sight."

"It runs in our family," Mitch told him.

They actually went to the concert.

She had her date: her Boston Pops concert at Symphony Hall.

They sat at little round tables on little rickety chairs, as if they were visiting a maiden aunt and having tea on the sun porch. The musicians gathered on a stage whose massive floral arrangements could probably be seen from Mars.

"What's your order?" said Mitch.

"What's my *order?*" she repeated. "I must be very punchy. After all, we haven't had any sleep in so long. Do you tell John Williams what you want him to perform? In that case, I'll have a *Jurassic Park* and an *Indiana Jones* please."

Mitch laughed. "Food, baby. Food before music."

From a form lying on the table, Mitch checked off roast beef sandwiches, two each, lemonade, and raspberry chocolate cake. A waitress in a cute little black and white outfit dashed over.

A symphony concert where you ate at the table. "I have definitely never been here before," she said. She thought of all the new things she would do with Mitch. As Lynne Cook.

"I bought you a present," Mitch said, as they devoured their food. All around them, people ate delicately, nibbling little crumbs off ladylike portions. Mitch and Lynne did nothing of the sort. They gobbled.

"When did you have time to go shopping?" she cried. "Mitch! You're a wizard." She ripped off the pretty paper.

Mitch loved that in a present-opener. When you opened neatly and slowly, you weren't having enough fun.

She yanked off the lid of the little white box and stared down into the layer of white cotton. "Mitch. I don't have pierced ears. You've been kissing them. You should have noticed that."

Sure enough, she did not have pierced ears. "Hmmm," said Mitch. This was familiar. He must be a slow learner.

She hung the earrings from the top buttonhole of her shirt. She was that kind of girl — she'd make anything work.

John Williams crossed the stage. The applause was deafening.

They moved their little chairs even closer together. They held hands. Lynne Cook, thought Mitch. I like that. It's a solid name.

But in secret, in his heart, part of her would always be Hope; for Hope, and the adventure she had given him, was unforgettable.

About the Author

Caroline B. Cooney lives in a small seacoast village in Connecticut. She writes every day on a word processor and then goes for a long walk down the beach to figure out what she's going to write the following day. She's written fifty books for young people, including *Forbidden, Flight #116 Is Down, The Party's Over, Saturday Night, Last Dance,* and *Summer Nights.* She reads as much as possible and has three grown children.